ESCAPE FROM
BILLY'S BAR-B-QUE

ESCAPE FROM BILLY'S BAR-B-QUE

JOANNE BRASIL

WILD TREES PRESS
NAVARRO, CALIFORNIA

ACKNOWLEDGMENTS

To John Hund, who, while employed as a mechanic more than 40 hours a week, also graciously volunteered to help me as critic and editorial consultant.

To Myrna Slade, who, though employed as a deli worker, has cooked me so many meals for the past five years that I can't even count them.

To Stephen Slade, who was the first to say it was a good idea, and who let me use his typewriter.

To Robert Allen, for his class-consciously sensitive editing, and loyal respect to the voice and integrity of Cecyl.

And last, but not least, to Alice Walker, who sent me a hug from her characters to mine, and who has made the publication of this book possible, as well as allowing me total artistic freedom, which means more than I can say.

And p.s.: To Mom and Dad, Mary Jane and Harold Goetkin, and to Sue, and Kakie, and Liz, my sisters, and to Phil, my brother because if it hadn't been for you I wouldn't be me. And to Dr. & Mrs. E.C. Kollman, and Elise and Jeff Harrison, and Mr. & Mrs. Vernon Goldsberry, who are also in my "family." If you weren't you, how could I be me?

—J.B.

Published by
Wild Trees Press
P.O. Box 378
Navarro, CA 95463

ISBN: 0-931125-01-4 (hardcover)
0-931125-02-2 (paperback)
Library of Congress Catalog Card: 85-051251

Cover art: "Fat Girl Complex"
(oil on canvas), by Carrie Scoville.
Reproduced by permission.
Cover design: Sarah Levin

Typeset and produced by Heyday Books,
Berkeley, CA
Printed and bound by Edwards Brothers,
Ann Arbor, MI

10 9 8 7 6 5 4 3 2 1

This Book Is Dedicated To:
Rosalie and Michelle Williams, and
to Victor

CONTENTS

Life in Phoebus

PHOEBUS, VIRGINIA is a little town, just big enough to support one X-rated movie theater, one dirty book store, one bank, one bakery (which has always used too much lard), one pawn shop, one library, two barber shops, and two bar-b-que places. My father owned one of the bar-b-que places, "Billy's Bar-B-Que."

Since they still had racial segregation then (which they still do now, too, of course), they needed to have two barber shops and two bar-b-que places so they could keep all the Black people and White people separate. They had two grocery stores, too, but everyone was allowed to shop at both of them. I don't know why. The White people just said that that's the way you were supposed to do it.

No Black people ever came into Billy's Bar-B-Que, but lots of White people did: workers from the cement factory, G.I.'s from Fort Monroe, fishermen, crabbers, and many others, mostly all men.

They'd come in and order a coke and french fries and a bar-b-que: the "Number One" (sliced pork slathered in bar-b-que sauce between two limp pieces of white bread that would get all orange and soggy), and the "Number Two" (chopped pork cooked in bar-b-que sauce for hours, maybe days, on hamburger buns with cole slaw and hot sauce). They were good.

We also sold gum, mints, cigarettes, cigarette holders, sanitized combs, "man-sized" handkerchiefs, baseball caps, and much, much more, including "personal hygiene products" for women. The personal hygiene products for women came in bright blue boxes that you could see all over the store, which was very embarrassing to me.

Billy's was just a normal little place. Everything was normal. Normal formica tables, normal chrome chairs, a normal counter, and a row of normal stools. There were normal travel posters of Las Vegas and Hawaii, too. The only thing that wasn't normal was Billy. The only thing that didn't belong at Billy's was Billy, Billy and the rest of us.

We immigrated to Phoebus from Shannon, Ireland when I was eight years old so that my father could go into business with Uncle Timothy (his brother) and Aunt Elizabeth. Uncle Timothy was a pharmacist; and during WWII, Uncle Timothy was sent by the Allies to Norfolk, Virginia, to the U.S. Naval Amphibious Weapons Station. He says it was just a mistake.

There in Norfolk, though, he met Aunt Elizabeth. He married her, and became a War Husband, never to return to his native land again. He didn't care.

Aunt Elizabeth was nobody special to most people since they didn't have Women's Liberation yet.

In 1955, Aunt Elizabeth and Uncle Tim decided to go into the pharmacy-with-a-soda-fountain business in Phoebus. They thought that Phoebus had "high rapid growth potential." They were wrong.

It wasn't long after we arrived in Phoebus that Uncle

Timothy and Aunt Elizabeth began to regret having moved to Phoebus, and moved back across the Hampton Roads Bay to Norfolk. Uncle Tim went to work for a drug store chain called "Four Star Discount Drugs," and was subsequently very pleased with his decision.

Phoebus never did grow. It's still the same now. My parents decided to stay in Phoebus even though Aunt Elizabeth and Uncle Tim left. They took out the pharmacy, since there wouldn't be any pharmacist without Uncle Tim. Then they expanded the soda-fountain and turned it into "Billy's Bar-B-Que." My father ("Theodore") named himself after it, and we all became Americans after that.

My father was proud to be in America and proud to be in business. He made more money that way, but that wasn't the whole reason why he stayed there in business so long, though. I think he stayed there so long just because he liked the customers so much. "Billy" would say that, as a businessman, it was his responsibility to have "good public relations." That's why he started giving away free empty jars to the Old Veterans who passed by on their way to the bootleg house. He declared that it was part of his program of "good public relations" as well as "Southern hospitality."

I was afraid of the Old Veterans because they were so dirty and spit a lot, but Billy said that many of the Old Veterans were so old and so sick and in such pain that if they wanted to wear old, dirty clothes, and spit, and smoke, and drink bootleg whiskey, it was nobody's business. They were "debilitated," Billy would say. He was right. To this day veterans are still debilitated and are in need of our support.

To show his support for the Old Veterans, then, Billy gave them free empty jars to take to the bootleg house. It was mostly only the Old Veterans with the debilitating injuries who went to the bootleg house. There were lots of these disabled men in Phoebus because there was a very large Veterans Administration Center Hospital nearby.

Sad to say, but the Old Veterans would hobble over to get

their corn liquor on crutches and in wheel chairs all the way from the Veterans Administration Center Hospital about two miles away. Sometimes they would stop by at Billy's for an empty jar.

They liked to tell jokes and stories with Billy. Billy would say that he, too, had been a veteran of heavy combat himself. Billy felt ashamed of himself because he was almost deaf in one ear and never was in any combat at all, so he told himself and everyone else, too, that he HAD been in some terrible fighting and that that's how he came to be deaf in one ear almost, from all the terrible bombs and artillery shelling.

Sometimes he would say that he had been a member of the British Royal Swamp Rats, Pup Tent #One, Military Order of the Cootie. This was not true; he just saw the words stamped inside a paper-back book that one Old Veteran (who never came back again) left on a chair at Billy's.

The bootleg house was just around the corner from Billy's on Segar Street. It was a normal-looking little gray shot-gun shack* just like any other shotgun shack except that there were two lights over the front porch. When the moonshine was ready, a green light would come on and a white one would go off. Then the Old Veterans would come around for their jars.

It was much cheaper to buy alcohol at the bootleg house than it was at the state liquor store, also known as the "packy," or "package store." You couldn't buy liquor by the drink in Virginia then, and I don't think you can now either unless you buy a meal also. They're funny about alcohol in The South.

In fact, a judge in Chatanooga, Tennessee even ruled once that a topless waitress could serve meals in a restaurant, but not alcoholic beverages. It can be that way in The

---

* A shot-gun shack is a small house composed of a line of rooms, built in a single file so straightly that a speeding bullet could pass through unimpeded. Similar to railroad apartments found in The North.

South. Anyway, Billy never went to the bootleg house because he didn't like corn liquor; he liked Schlitz beer. What he liked best was to sit on the front porch of our little house and drink Schlitz beer.

The problem was that there were two members of the Women's Christian Temperance Union ("WCTU") living next door. Even though it was the end of the 1950's by then, the WCTU was still going strong in some parts of the South.

Billy correctly supposed that they wouldn't like to see him sitting on the front porch with his Schlitz beer, and so he put up a trellis and grew several varieties of ivy over it. Until the ivy grew in, Billy just poured his Schlitz beer into a coffee cup so that nobody could see what he was drinking. Then the Old Ladies worried, instead, that he was drinking too much coffee, and started making him batches of mint tea. He didn't like it, though.

My mother, who eventually was known in our family in America as "Mom," never drank at all. She liked the mint tea, and drank it all. She was, and still is, a Virgo, astrological sign of health and purification. She often bought Schlitz beer at the grocery store for Billy, though.

Mom was a housewife. She stayed home and took care of us and invented Southern recipes for the "Daily Special" at Billy's Bar-B-Que. There was a new Southern dish every day besides bar-b-que: fried pork sandwiches with red-eye gravy, crab burgers, Vienna sausage biscuits. Nowadays they say that almost everything used in making Southern food is bad for you: pork, pork fat, white flour, salt, iced tea with lots of sugar is all said to be very bad, but back then it didn't seem to bother anyone at all.

My parents struggled hard to be good Americans and good Southerners. The worst time, though, was when Mom was trying to speak with a Southern accent. She would say things like, "I'm *fixing* to go to the store," things Aunt Elizabeth would say. But when Mom said them, they sounded wrong, and she had to stop. Billy kept trying and trying, though, trying to fit in. I guess Mom and Billy somehow did fit in after a while. I never did fit in, though. I never did adjust at all to living in Phoebus. I don't know why.

My worst times were in school. I never could understand what I was supposed to think, that was the trouble. I never did think like I was supposed to think, and that meant that I could *do* something wrong any minute, and not even know it.

The worst trouble started in sixth grade. Our teacher, Mrs. Matt, gave us a history lesson on slavery in the Old South. In order to be as "unbiased" as possible, Mrs. Matt carefully divided the blackboard into two equal parts. On one side we were supposed to list the "Bad" things about slavery in the Old South, and on the other side, we were supposed to list the "Good" things about it.

I can't remember what all the good and bad things were, but I do remember that Betty Baines, my best friend, thought of the first good thing: "It Christianized the heathen African," Betty said. "That's right, Betty," said Mrs. Matt, and she wrote it on the board: "C...h...r...i...s...t ianized the heathen African." Mrs. Matt knew about these things because her husband was a Christian minister.

In sixth grade, Betty Baines got to be my best and only friend, and that was because she lived closer to me than anyone else; she lived upstairs, directly over Billy's Bar-B-Que.

One day Betty and I were walking home from school. We always passed a yellow school bus full of Black children at the same time at that same place because we always went the same way at the same time. Betty always told me to hide my eyes, and not to look whatever I did.

I did what she told me for a long time, but one day I couldn't resist any longer. I looked. They were all giving us The Finger. I thought that this was a very terrible thing, and I haven't ever, even to this day, looked at people on buses again.

One thing about Betty Baines, she was never confused, especially when it came to being White. She knew just what to do. The thing was, Betty took it for granted that she was White, I didn't.

I don't know what caused the trouble, but I never felt very secure in my Whiteness. I looked White. Everyone in my family was White. I used the Whites Only drinking fountains, bathrooms, movie theaters, and the front of the bus. Still I had a lingering insecure feeling that there was something wrong, some flaw in my Whiteness. I just didn't FEEL White. I didn't feel Black, either. But I didn't have that same feeling of Whiteness that the other White people seemed to have.

I used to feel very odd every time I loked out the window of Billy's Bar-B-Que in the direction of Big Mamma's Barber Shop, which was right across the street from Billy's. Big Mamma's was the Black barbershop. I was not allowed to cross over to that side of the street. Billy said, "You have no business going over there." But I knew from staring into Big Mamma's picture window so many times that there was a small transitor radio that Big Mamma kept in a cigar box behind the counter.

Sometimes Big Mamma's friends would come over, and if it weren't busy, they'd dance around and have a lot of fun. Big Mamma wouldn't dance, but she would move her head around on her neck in a certain way that was very wonderful and talented. I watched the dancing through the window a lot. I also watched dance contests on TV every day after school with Betty Baines.

Every day after school Betty Baines and I would do our chores, she at home for her mother, and I at Billy's for Billy. Then I'd go upstairs with her to her house and watch dance contests on TV. We watched and we practiced. It seemed to us that we were getting pretty good, and I longed to go over to Big Mamma's and practice steps with Big Mamma's friends. I suppose this is all very racist. Almost anything anyone says about anyone of another race is usually racist I guess. I suppose it's not really polite to even talk about another race at all because you might not know what you are talking about, and besides, it's none of your business.

I do admit, though, that I still have a desire to go over to Big Mamma's and get out the transistor radio and dance with everyone there. This is now a tragically hopeless desire because Big Mamma's is out of business, and I shall never again have the chance to go over there in my life, although I never had a chance to go there before either. I shall, in fact, probably never get to see Big Mamma again as long as I live, and I'm quite sure that Big Mamma could care less and never has, or at least it's very unlikely.

It used to be my daydream though, that one day Big Mamma would come over to Billy's Bar-B-Que, and I'd say hello and give her a free sandwich, just like Billy would do for the other merchants in town, the White ones, that is. But now that dream will never come true.

Well, on the other corners of the intersection where Billy's Bar-B-Que was (the intersection of Mellon and County Streets), there was only one other corner that I was allowed to cross over to (I couldn't cross over to the pawn shop, either, but I didn't want to), and that was the corner with the Public Library. I went there every day to read magazines.

I knew, then, that they were having "integration" in The South. In Phoebus they didn't have integration at all, but I thought that this was because Phoebus was too *run down* to have integration. But it was true that they were having it in Hampton, Virginia, the next town over.

The thing about Hampton was that they had a very large, predominantly Black college, Hampton Institute, there.

Hampton Institute was originally a school for Indians and for freed slaves, and there are many old, historical photographs of this time that you can see now at the college museum.

Nowadays many students at Hampton Institute take

great pride in wearing Gucci shoes, but in those days of civil rights, the students at Hampton Institute (some of them) put more emphasis on political activity than on imported shoes. At that time, many students from Hampton Institute were beginning to participate in "sit-down strikes."

That meant that they would go into a previously all-White establishment of some sort: a restaurant or a church, for example. Then they would sit down, even though this had never been done by Blacks in White places ever before. It was another turn in history, but it did nothing to provide the Black people with Gucci shoes. Nowadays I think more students from Hampton Institute are more interested in preparing to sit down in corporate executive offices.

Anyway, one day some of the students at Hampton Institute decided to have a sit-down strike at the soda fountain at Liggit's Rexall Drugs in Hampton. They did, in fact, go into Liggit's and sit down. Mr. Liggit, as the paper reported, was "fit to be tied." For the next two years, he refused to serve any food to anyone at that soda fountain. Not a thing. Just nothing. Not a grilled cheese sandwich or a Dr. Pepper, just nothing. Finally he took all the seats off the stools, every one of them.

For two years, then, all there was in the front of Liggit's Rexall Drugs was an empty lunch counter and a row of seatless, naked, stainless steel posts sticking up in the air.

I thought the students and everyone else would come in and eat at Billy's Bar-B-Que then, but they didn't. I can't remember what happened after that, but I do know that if you went into Liggit's Rexall Drug Store now, you could sit down wherever you wanted to sit at that soda fountain, no matter who you were, provided that you could pay for what you ordered.

If you went there today, in fact, you could see all kinds of people, Black and White, sitting down and eating and drinking coffee, and ruining their lungs with cigarettes—all in the same room together, Blacks and Whites. And nobody seems to mind at all, except for a few non-smokers who have recently begun to campaign for a separate, segregated, non-smoking section.

I don't know why, but none of the students from Hampton Institute ever came over to Billy's Bar-B-Que, even though it was only a half a mile away from Hampton Institute. They just didn't. In Phoebus, everything stayed pretty much the same all the time. The Black people still don't usually go into White bar-b-que places (although they do do this in Hampton, just the next town over), and Phoebus is still not noticeably becoming any kind of rapid growth area.

One day something interesting almost happened in Phoebus, though. It was a hot afternoon and a bus load of Freedom Riders were travelling through town when the engine over-heated. The bus came to a dead halt, sputtering and steaming like crazy, right between Big Mamma's and Billy's Bar-B-Que. This particular bus of Freedom Riders was enroute to Alabama or Mississippi or somewhere to participate in civil rights activities there, and was supposed to stop at Hampton Institute to take on more passengers.

All the Freedom Riders on the bus were staring out the windows, and all the people from Big Mamma's and Billy's Bar-B-Que came out and stared back. Finally the driver managed to drive the bus into the vacant lot in back of the pawn shop so that it could get out of the intersection, even though there wasn't much traffic.

By coincidence the pawn shop just happened to be open, and everyone could see all the guns inside. So could all the other people who followed the bus around the corner. The driver opened the hood of the engine. More steam escaped and more people gathered around. The driver wanted to look at the mechanical parts to see what was wrong and the people wanted to look at the driver to see if he were Black or White. (They couldn't tell which race he was because he turned out to be an in-between color. This was very important to everyone.)

Finally the driver went into the Pawn Shop and called a mechanic from Hampton Institute to come over and help. We all waited and waited, and finally a mechanic from Hampton Institute came over and fixed it, and then the bus went away with the driver and all the passengers. When the Freedom Riders were gone, everyone else went away, too, and the vacant lot in back of the pawn shop went back to normal again. I went back to Billy's Bar-B-Que to finish my chores for Billy and Mom.

I Move to the North

AFTER I FINISHED high-school I decided to move away from Phoebus and live in the The North. I guess I just wasn't the type to go to college or something, and there just wasn't anything too much more to do in Phoebus. I would have just spent more time filling up salt and peppers or hanging around with Betty Baines.

So I decided to go to The North, mainly because it would be something different, like going to a foreign country. I thought of the Freedom Riders and all the people in the bus that broke down in back of the pawn shop. I should have known that there was something wrong with The North as well as The South, though, because otherwise, if it was so good in The North, why didn't the Freedom Rider people just stay up there and send down the money for the Black people in The South to go be up there with them.

Mom and Billy said why in the world did I want to go to Boston. They said why didn't I want to go to Hawaii or some

place pretty and warm, with palm trees and stuff. I knew
they would not understand about my curiosity about The
North, so I just said that it would so be pretty in Boston, too,
and that if you wanted to get warm, all you would have to do
was go inside. And I said that they had a lot of museums in
Boston and it would be very cultural also.

So I went to Boston. It was as far North as I could afford
to go on my savings from my salary that Mom and Billy gave
me. Of course, they gave me a little extra money, too,
because maybe I was even going away forever or who knows
what; but mainly I knew that I would have to be on my own
and make my own money.

When I first got on the bus I was terribly sad. I was glad
that I could sit in a seat by myself because I started crying
when the bus pulled away from the depot in Phoebus. Well,
it wasn't really a depot, but it was just a spot in the road; but
when the bus pulled away from the spot on the road I just sat
there on the bus and could feel these tears starting to roll
down my cheeks, and I just let them roll down. I knew I was
never going back to Phoebus again for some reason, except
maybe to visit or something. But I knew it would never be
the same again, and I knew that this would be the end of
something.

Mainly it was all right, though. I got out my snacks that
Mom and Billy had packed me for the trip. And after I
stopped crying I sat and ate and ate. I was sitting there on
the bus thinking about food, and there were two women
sitting there in back of me thinking about food, too. I didn't
notice them for a while, but they started talking so loudly
that I couldn't help overhearing everything they said.
Besides, it felt better to think about strangers than to think
about Mom and Billy. And so I just kept on listening to
everything they said:

"You can't go wrong with a roast. Mmm-mmm. No ma'am.
I'll serve 'em a roast, that's what I'll do."

"That's a grand idea. And do y'ever make up a batch a

chili? Just to have it around for 'em? You know."

Looking out the window I noticed signs for McDonalds (speaking of food) and for Coca-Cola or Dr. Pepper; but there were not that many signs for bar-b-que places. Hardly any at all. Almost none.

When I got to Boston, I went to the YWCA Hotel. I had enough money to live on at the "Y" for about one month. At the "Y" everything smelled like mothballs, ammonia, and mildew. I felt that I was being punished for something here at the "Y," but I couldn't understand what it was that I was being punished for.

I missed Mom and Billy and our house with the ivy grown over the porch so much. It made me even kind of sick when I thought about it, and so I just had to put them all out of my mind, everything about Mom and Billy and Phoebus, right out of my mind. I thought about getting a job instead.

Every day I would go out and look for a job. I liked walking around the city so much. Still, out in the city, it seemed that no matter how glad I was to see anybody, nobody was ever very glad to see me. I still felt like I'd done something wrong every time I went somewhere, and still nobody would tell me what I had done. I tried to think of how to improve myself, but I couldn't.

One thing that I didn't realize at the time, though, that I do realize now, is that many people in The North think that people (both Black and White), who have Southern accents are stupid. This is really a very unfair prejudice, and it would have hurt my feelings terribly had I realized what was going on, which I did not, as I did speak with a very slight Southern accent at that time.

In addition to having a very slight Southern accent, my only work experience was "Waitress, Billy's Bar-B-Que." People would act like there was no such place, and even managers of pizza restaurants, which aren't the greatest places to eat in the world always, would look at me funny when I wrote that down on my application. There were lots of pizza restaurants in Boston, but I could not find one that wanted to hire me. Things started looking kind of bad.

At the end of my one month at the "Y" I couldn't afford my room any more, and I moved. I moved to a cheap rooming house on The Fenway. I got my room at the rooming house for free in exchange for being the janitor. Mom and Billy would have been terribly ashamed of me for taking out trash for strangers and everything I guess, but it was the best I could do.

It was mostly only Old Pensioners who lived on the Fenway, pensioners and music students. "The Fenway" is a piece of land that is located behind the Museum of Fine Arts in Boston. I guess it must have used to be very lovely and natural, but now it's all rotten and full of unnatural- smelling waste material, and is full of rats, killers, muggers, and rapists. That is often where they go.

Here on Hemenway (that's where the rooming house was) Street in The Fenway area of Boston I met my first friend, Mrs. Potter. Mrs. Potter was 85 years old, but she was friendly anyway. She had been living in her room there for nine years. Still, she didn't have any nick-knacks or much of anything at all to her name. She had been living in the the Fenway area for over twenty years. She said that her kids never came to see her, but that she used to have fun in the Old Days when they still had Easter Parades and everyone walked around in their hats and their special outfits.

Mrs. Potter, still, was more interested in The Hippies who kept moving into the neighborhood than anything else. Mr. Cranworthy, Mrs. Potter's neighbor across the hall, told Mrs. Potter that they were called "Hippies," and that more of them were moving to The Fenway all the time so that they could go to the music school and be rock and roll players.

One day Mrs. Potter and Mr. Cranworthy and I spent all afternoon watching the hippies across the street moving in. I guess we should have helped them, but Mrs. Potter and Mr. Cranworthy were too old, and I thought that I should

keep them company. But I know I should have helped the
Hippies anyway. But anyway, Mrs. Potter counted each one
out loud, each mattress: "25, 26, 27." Twenty-seven mat-
tresses. No box springs, no headboards. No tables and
no chairs. We sat together on folding chairs in front of
Mrs. Potter's window until the very last one had been
dragged up.

Mrs. Potter thought it was funny, but Mr. Cranworthy
said it was disgusting, and he just turned off his hearing aid
after a while, and pretended it wasn't working, which is what
he did when he got sick of everyone, which was most of
the time.

Mrs. Potter kept on watching the Hippies every day, and
giving reports. One day she reported that there were "male
and female Hippies together in the same sleeping rooms."
But later she changed her story and said that she just thought
this must be true, but she didn't know for sure.

Then she said that she thought there were Black Hippies,
too, but only male ones. Furthermore, she reported, "many
of the Black male Hippies go with White girls." But that was
all she knew.

Mrs. Potter wished that she knew more, though. She
wished that she could go ask somebody and find out more.
Finally she said to me, "Cecyl," (that's my name) "Cecyl,
don't you know something about this? Certainly you must
know something of your own generation?"

Unfortunately, I did not know anything of my generation. All I could say to Mrs. Potter was that where I came
from the Black people and the White people were nearly
always totally separated, and that I had always thought that
it was against the law for men and women to sleep in the
same place together and have sex no matter what race they
were. I told her that people could even be arrested right in
their bed if they slept together and had sex if they weren't
married, and that it was also illegal to marry someone of the
opposite race. But Mrs. Potter said this was not true.

I did not say this to Mrs. Potter, but personally I also thought that it must be very strange to sleep with a man, any man. It even seemed like a strange idea to me to go into a bar with a man and have a cocktail, although to everyone else in the world this seemed to be the normalest thing ever. I guess that was because Virginia was a "dry state" back then, and so having cocktails in bars was against the law, too, in addition to fornication.

I guess most everything in life seemed strange to me. The only normal thing was sitting with Mrs. Potter on her bench while she fed pigeons.

I didn't like pigeons because they flew in your face and made bird poop all over, even on your head, which did happen to me one time. But I liked to sit with Mrs. Potter when she fed them. She said that it was good for Old Ladies to feed pigeons because it gave them something useful to do with their time, and then they could talk to the other people who were also feeding them.

It was good for me, too, because I wasn't so homesick for Mom and Billy then. I felt silly still getting homesick as old as I was and everything. Anyway, I never did get to have a grandmother before I met Mrs. Potter because mine all died. One even died in The Blitz in London, and another had a stroke, and all my Grandpas died before I was born, too. My parents weren't very lucky.

Anyway, one day while we were feeding the pigeons, one of the Hippie Girls from across the street came out and joined us. Mrs. Potter was very excited to meet her first Hippie Girl. The Hippie Girl was very nice, and answered all of Mrs. Potter's questions about the Hippie Apartment. I was excited also.

Mrs. Potter felt that it would be all right to ask the Hippie Girl the big question, the One Biggest Question that she had been dying to ask for so long: "Do you ever go with Blacks?"

I was mortally embarrassed. I cringed and waited for something just awful to happen, but it didn't. The Hippie

Girl just said, "Yes." I saw the look on Mrs. Potter's face. I just knew she couldn't leave well enough alone, and I just knew that Mrs. Potter was going to say something else. She said, "Why?"

I thought somebody would faint dead away. I was pretty sure that the Hippie Girl would be very outraged and slap Mrs. Potter's face or something, but she didn't. She just said "because they're nicer." I turned beet red, and Mrs. Potter just sat there saying, "nicer," "nicer."

I knew what was going on in Mrs. Potter's mind. She was wandering in her mind back to The War. She did this all the time. She would go back to the time they made her go to work in a propeller factory. She said she liked it by the end of her time there, but by that time The War was over, and she had to stop because The Men were coming home except for Mr. Potter who was killed.

Mrs. Potter always seemed so far away when she talked about The War. It seemed like a thing in her mind that was not really real, but she said that it had been a real thing, and that she had "competence" in her work in the propeller factory, but that this work never came back, like Mr. Potter.

I couldn't understand it very well because I never had a husband or competence in my work, either, just filling up ketchup bottles and scrubbing floors and all. So I'd just listen when she talked about this.

Mrs. Potter said she always expected to find another husband and another kind of competence in some other kind of work, but she never did. Mrs. Potter said that she never did yet find a man that she thought would be a really "nice" companion for her old age, but that she hadn't given up.

She used to tell me about all the men she knew. She'd talk about every one of them, and make a list in her mind of all the qualities, good and bad, that they had. But she never could come up with one that she could say to herself was really and truly "nice." And this is why when the Hippie Girl said that the Black men were "nicer," Mrs. Potter had to stop and think.

The Hippie Girl came back to Mrs. Potter's bench again and again. And again and again Mrs. Potter would ask all kinds of questions. It seemed like the Hippie Girl, somehow, was lonely even though she lived with twenty-six or so other people. It seemed impossible, and so Mrs. Potter kept asking all these questions, just trying to figure it out. It seemed kind of sad.

Gradually, the Hippie Girl got to be our good friend, my first friend in Boston my own age. One day the Hippie Girl invited me and Mrs. Potter to a party her boyfriend was giving. Mrs. Potter jumped at the chance, but I made up excuses about why I would be unable to attend, and Mrs. Potter called me "an old lady."

Mrs. Potter made sure we were the first people there. She loved it. I hated it, being the first. Mrs. Potter loved everything. After people arrived, and it was clear that most of the men were Black and most of the girls (as we used to say) were White, even then Mrs. Potter continued to love it all, while I began to slink back into a corner. Mrs. Potter, pulling me out of my corners, talked to as many of the guests as she could, however.

She was the only person there who was so old and had so much gray hair and so many wrinkles, but she didn't seem to mind standing out at all. A fellow with a huge black Afro, wearing nothing but a pair of lime green satin pants asked Mrs. Potter to dance. She did. I guess the fellow got sick of how Mrs. Potter was dancing, though, because finally he told her to "quit flappin' your arms and legs like you was a chicken."

The fellow showed Mrs. Potter some steps that he was doing. After a while she started to get the hang of it, and came over and dragged me out with them. I was very embarrassed, and felt that everyone was staring right through to my bones. This was not true, of course, I don't think. But I tried to dance a little anyway, since Mrs. Potter was making me.

After a few minutes I got to having a good time, too. It

ime since the days when Betty Baines and I had
front of the TV, and I found that all our
practice sessions had paid off. I knew all the steps that the
fellow, who was calling himself "Crawdaddy," was showing
Mrs. Potter. It was very embarrassing, but Crawdaddy
called me and Mrs. Potter his "team." We even got several
routines organized, which were almost a hit. Well, kind of a
hit. At least, I could stop being embarrassed. It seemed like
everyone could do whatever they wanted and nobody got
embarrassed. I liked this feeling.

When the party was over Crawdaddy drove me and Mrs.
Potter home. This was his idea of social courtesy, he said, to
drive the ladies home; the only thing was, we only lived
around the corner. Still, even though we only lived around
the corner, and his car was parked further away than that,
he said it was only common courtesy to give us a ride home.

On the way home, he stopped at an all-night cafeteria
down the street and bought me and Mrs. Potter "dropped
eggs on English" as they used to say all the time in Boston
at the all-night cafeterias. I myself didn't like dropped
(poached) eggs on English (muffins), and I was getting
homesick for Billy's Bar-B-Que for some reason, but I ate
mine anyway to be polite.

When we finally got home I was very depressed and tired
and homesick. I hated my dropped eggs. They felt all slimey.
And when we got out of the car Crawdaddy asked Mrs.
Potter for our phone number, the number of the telephone
in the hall. I didn't want to give it to him, and so I said I
didn't have a phone; but Mrs. Potter gave him the hall
number anyway. I thought Mrs. Potter was being pretty
dumb, but I didn't say anything just to be polite.

Somehow or other I got to be Crawdaddy's girlfriend. I
don't know how that happened, but I kept going out with
him and Mrs. Potter. Then I was just going out with him,
just to be polite in case he thought I was prejudiced. Then I
just started getting used to him, and then I got to like him

and got a crush on him. It was embarrassing, but I didn't know how someone was supposed to act when they were someone's girlfriend, especially if it was a person of the opposite race's girlfriend I was supposed to be being.

For one thing, I was never a beauty parlor type too much. Even when I have gone into the beauty parlor I would just look worse when I came out. And even when I came out of the beauty parlor looking OK, it still wasn't the way I really looked; it wasn't the way I felt. It was just the way the beauty operator felt. And so I quit bothering. Besides I couldn't afford it.

After a little while I figured that I, too, could be a Hippie Girl. I started copying everything the Hippie Girl did. I ironed my hair and wore short skirts and got a black eye-liner pencil and started saying, "oh, wow," when I couldn't think of anything good to say. It worked out all right.

One day the hall phone rang, and it was not Crawdaddy. It was Betty Baines. She wanted to know if she could come and stay with me because she wanted to come live in The North, too. I said she could but I was kind of poor. She said that was OK, but I couldn't tell anyone that she was there, not even Mom or Billy. I said OK and I didn't ask her why in order to be polite.

Betty Baines
Moves to the North, Too

THERE WAS SOMETHING about talking to Betty Baines on the phone that kind of made my brain stop working. Plus, I got nervous because it was expensive. I wasn't used to talking on the phone long distance, so when Betty Baines called up those few times, there were lots of things I forgot to ask her about. But she said Mom and Billy were fine, and everyone was fine, and everything in Phoebus was just the same.

I told her that I was a janitor, and that there was an extra cot and that we could get her a recovered mattress at the Goodwill. I told Betty Baines that I wouldn't tell Mom and Billy even that she was here if she wouldn't tell Mom and Billy that I was a Hippie now and that I had a Negro boyfriend. She said she wouldn't but I could tell that she thought I was in terrible trouble. I guess you could look at it that way.

Betty Baines got a ride with a friend of hers part way to

Boston and then she took a bus the rest of the way. When she arrived in Boston she looked pretty tired. She looked at my room and looked at my roominghouse and looked pretty depressed, but she didn't say anything bad in order to be polite. Crawdaddy came and took us to the all-night cafeteria, and I could tell Betty Baines was getting kind of scared, but she didn't say anything impolite still. Then one day she got used to it and she said, "Gee, Cecyl, this is kind of weird here." "Yeah," I said, "It is."

After Betty had been in Boston a month or so she started getting pretty fat. I didn't want to say anything because it wouldn't have been polite, but finally she said, "Cecyl, guess what." I couldn't guess what, of course, so she says, "Cecyl, guess what, promise you won't tell anyone." So I said, yes, OK, I would not tell and then she said (of course), "Cecyl, guess what, I'm pregnant."

I forgot to be polite and said, "Betty! You're kidding me!" But she wasn't. She was pregnant for real. She got bigger and bigger. When she got real big she refused to leave our room ever. She was so embarrassed. She just stayed in all the time or went to Mrs. Potter's room.

Mrs. Potter was very nice to Betty. She said she could tell Betty was pregnant by the look in her eye and that she knew all along what was going on, and she also said that she never had gotten to be a grandmother and wouldn't that be nice. She even persuaded Betty to call up her Mom and Dad and tell them where she was. Mrs. Potter persuaded Betty to call up her Mom and Dad, even, and tell them that she was going to have a baby.

Mrs. Potter said, "Betty, they'll understand, you'll see. You don't give your parents enough credit for loving you." Mrs. Potter was wrong. Betty Baines called up her Mom and Dad. She told them that she was pregnant and she was ashamed of herself and that's why she came all the way up here. She told them that she was going to have a baby. Betty's parents were not understanding at all. They told her that she should be ashamed and that it was good that she went up to The North to hide her shame, and not to come back down there and shame them with it whatever she did. So she didn't ever go back again. And that's how it was that Betty Baines and I had a baby together. We didn't plan it that way, it just happened.

For a long time Betty didn't know what to do: have it adopted or keep it. Mrs. Potter kept saying keep it. I even said keep it and we could raise it up by ourselves if she didn't mind being a little bit poor. Betty said that she wanted her baby to be better off, though, and maybe they could find a nice rich person to adopt it.

Even Crawdaddy was being pretty nice about it. He even said keep it and we could all raise it up together. Everyone seemed happy about it except Betty Baines. She stuck to her guns that she wanted her baby to be better off, and went off to an adoption agency. The rest of us didn't know what to say, and a social worker from the state started coming around to look at our rooming house.

The social worker even turned out to be nice, and she got Betty some free money so that she could have her own room and her own bed in our roominghouse. Still, Betty didn't feel happy about being pregnant. She refused to go out at all when she got towards the end, and all that she ever did was sit around and eat. She ate so much finally that she got toxemia and had to go to the hospital.

While Betty was in the hospital, I thought my life would go back to normal. I thought I'd go back to visiting Mrs. Potter on her bench, taking out the trash, and going out with Crawdaddy sometimes. But my life did not go back to normal altogether because Crawdaddy started being very mean to me. Mrs. Potter said that she was "gratified" to know that it was not true in every case that "the Black Male was nicer than the White Male." Every person's an individual.

My life wasn't really ruined, but my life seemed ruined to

me. All that was really ruined was that I quit seeing Crawdaddy, and that was probably just fine. It seemed like my life
was ruined for sure, though.

All I was doing then was going to visit Betty Baines at Holy
Shrine Hospital, and it was way out at the end of the MTA
subway line in Jamaica Plain. I'd just sit there on the MTA
train and stare out the window when we got above ground.
It seemed like Betty was in there taking care of her toxemia
forever.

By the time I'd get out to Holy shrine Hospital I'd be in a
funny kind of a mood, and there Betty Baines would be
sitting up in her comfortable hospital bed, just watching TV
and eating. Betty never did quit her over-eating when she
was pregnant, but sometimes when I came to visit her in the
hospital she'd give me her dinner when nobody was looking
so I'd be cheered up. I knew that Betty could always find a
way to get some more food even though she wasn't supposed to. I always seemed to look more sickly than Betty
after she went to the hospital, and I guess I shouldn't have
eaten Betty Baines' dinners, but I did, and I didn't even feel
bad about it.

One day I went out to Holy Shrine Hospital to see Betty. I
brought her a submarine sandwich for dinner, and she gave
me her pork chops and creamed corn. Betty said she had
some good news for me. She said she was going to go into
labor very soon, she could tell, and that she decided to keep
the baby.

I was so surprised. I said was she sure, and was it OK with
the people who were going to adopt it and everything. And
she said that she knew the people would be sad, but that she
could change her mind. Betty told this to the social worker
and it all worked out OK, and Betty was allowed to change
her mind even though the other people would be real sad
and have to get another baby and everything. All Betty had
to do was fill out a whole bunch of more papers.

I had to go out right away and find us an apartment

because the social worker said that Betty could not live in the rooming-house with a baby because of the Welfare laws. I found us an apartment over in Cambridge where I could be a janitor and Betty could live on Welfare. I thought the manager of the building would think badly of me and Betty for being a janitor and a Welfare person, but he just said he didn't care where the Holy Jesus the money came from as long as he got it on time. I didn't think that he was a very nice person at all, but I gave him our money, which was just about everything we had, anyway. He just said, "Hey, you pay-a the money, you get-a the key." He thought he was so funny.

Finally the baby came out. Mrs. Potter was there. I was there. We were both there. Of course, it was still the Old Days and we could not go into the delivery room, but we did stay there near the door in the hallway. A nurse finally came out after hours and hours and told us, "it's a girl." Little Peggy had finally come out of Betty Baines. Mrs. Potter and I stood there just hopping up and down, we were so happy about little Peggy.

When Betty and Peggy got out of the hospital, we moved over to our new apartment in Cambridge. Mrs. Potter said that she would be real lonesome without us, but just as long as she could come over sometimes and be the Granny, she'd be happy anyways. But even though I was happy and Mrs. Potter was kind of happy, Betty Baines still looked like something was wrong. She'd been in Holy Shrine Hospital so long that I forgot about how bad she was feeling sometimes.

Here I went and found us an apartment in a building where I could be the janitor and she could live on Welfare, and I got over Crawdaddy. I thought everything would be OK, but Betty was still feeling funny. She said that it was a feeling called "post partum depression" that was bothering her, but it was different from that. Betty was still ashamed.

Betty was still so ashamed that she didn't want to take the

baby, her very own little Peggy, out into public view. She just stayed home all the time all depressed and dejected looking. She was still feeling bad. Finally she came out with it, though, and said, "Oh, Cecyl, I'm so ashamed of myself, what will anybody think of me?" But then we figured out that we could just say that Betty's husband was killed in Viet Nam, and that I was her sister from Virginia who came up to keep her company. Betty even bought herself a gold band, and started to believe her widow story her own self. This made her feel better. Mrs. Potter came over a lot and we called her "granny," and this helped Betty Baines believe that she did, too, have a family that loved her. But Betty Baines own real family did not really love her anymore, and they never even once defrosted their cold, cold hearts even long enough to come and see their own little dear darling Peggy. Hard to believe though it is.

Come to think of it, my own Mom and Billy never came to see me either, but I always figured that they were very busy with the restaurant and all.

I don't know if the people around us in Cambridge ever believed that Betty was a widow and I was her real sister or not. I don't think that people around us in Cambridge even cared at all.

As I had read so often in the magazines at the Phoebus Public Library, the young people in Cambridge were busy creating a "cultural revolution." And even though Betty Baines and I were both Post-War Babies, too, I didn't understand what the other Post-War Babies were all about. That was because I was not a college student. Instead, I was a janitor or a sister or a kind of a related person that there wasn't any name for, and I lived in a place where I cleaned up all the time and where we had a little tiny baby that cried a lot. It was different for us.

Sometimes me and Betty would take Peggy out walking on nice days. We'd go past Harvard University buildings and people, past M.I.T. buildings and people. We'd see all

the college students in their blue jeans and long hair. They
looked just like me and Betty Baines, all right. They were
the same age and everything, and there were thousands of
them everywhere.

Post War Babies
and Their Habits and Habitat

MOST OF THE Post-War Babies in Cambridge seemed to live in dirty Yankee tenements, the kinds of places the people in Phoebus warned me about: cold, barren, dirty, and expensive. You wouldn't believe it, they said. They were right.

The Post-War Babies, or Hippies, lived in some ways a lot like the slaves did in the Old South. I could remember it from Mrs. Matt's history lessons from sixth grade:

1. They lived in over-crowded housing.
2. They lived together, men and women, and bore children without benefit of marriage, although some married.
3. They hardly ever ate meat except pork fat.
4. They were split up from their true families.

One thing that made them different from the slaves of the Old South, though, was that it seemed like they went anywhere they wanted to go. They had lots of trucks and cars and buses that they would paint up in loud, garish colors. When Betty Baines and Peggy and I went out walking, the Post-War Baby Hippies would give us the Peace Sign, and offer us to smoke some "reefer" with them.

We got to be friendly with some Post-War Baby Hippies who lived in our building, Betty and I did. As always they gave us the Peace Sign and offered us to smoke some reefer. Betty never did smoke any reefer, but one day I did. It made my throat get really dry and scratchy because I wasn't used to smoking anything at all.

When I came back home with my voice all low and scratchy, Betty Baines got scared and told me don't act crazy or she'll hit me with a frying pan. Then she stared at me a lot to see what I would do, but I didn't do anything different.

It seemed to me that all reefer did was slow down the people in The North who were always rushing around so fast. It only seemed to make them normal again, and I couldn't see what everybody thought the big deal was. Of course, it did make ME a little bit *too* slow because I wasn't used to being in The North and rushing around anyway, so I didn't need any slowing down at all.

There were lots of Post-War Babies and Hippies in our building, it turned out. They told me and Betty that we were "beautiful" and "far out." They loved to do goo goo eyes at Peggy, and they were always offering to baby-sit; but Betty Baines wouldn't let them because they might smoke reefer and start asking "what is real?" and stuff like that or start reading *Finnegan's Wake* out loud even though they said they didn't get it at all. Betty Baines said that she didn't ever want to hear about them reading that stuff to Peggy and warp her mind and everything she said.

The Hippies upstairs were always trying to get Betty stoned so they could read *Finnegan's Wake* to her. They were called "drop outs." They didn't understand that Betty Baines hadn't ever dropped IN in the first place. She just didn't enjoy these things at all. Furthermore, she would say to me all the time, she had too much responsibility with being a Mom and that she was sick of getting up in the middle of the night. I felt bad then because I never did get up in the middle of the night, although I did do about everything else for little Peggy, including rinse out poopy diapers. But it was true, I never got up to give her a bottle. I was selfish.

Betty and I stayed there in that building in that apartment for about a year and a half. I'd take out the trash and sweep and clean and paint walls when people moved out, and Betty would get up in the middle of the night. We both baby-sat.

I felt so happy like that. I could do almost anything I wanted to. But Betty got fed up. She said there was more to life than that. That hurt my feelings because I thought we had such a nice life there. I couldn't picture what could be better. We had lots of friends right there in our building, and I liked it when they read books out loud that I couldn't understand, but Betty said she wanted more out of life.

Finally Betty did get something more out of life. She got a stockbroker. He moved into our building. I cleaned it and painted it and everything like usual. At first he seemed to be so very poor. I invited him over to dinner sometimes. He liked Betty right away but the sad thing was that Betty would do whatever he said to do.

If she were in the middle of eating her dinner one night and he called and asked her to eat dinner with him, she'd even go into the bathroom and throw up so she could eat with him all over again. I didn't see what there was to be so excited about, but I guess it wasn't my business.

It broke my heart when Betty moved in with the stock-broker, but Mrs. Potter said that's what Betty wanted all along, to be respectable. Betty and the stock broker even got married in a church. Mrs. Potter and I and Peggy all came along. After all, we were her only relatives alive because her husband got killed in Viet Nam and her parents were killed in a car crash.

Mrs. Potter said don't feel bad because Betty and Peggy

were only right upstairs, and I could see them all the time, and everything would work out, I'd see. It didn't. The stockbroker got richer and richer, and then they moved out of our building altogether and into a better place. Finally they moved to a really, really fancy building in New York City and I never saw Betty or Peggy again.

After Betty Baines moved out my first room mate was Barbara Halberstrom. Barbara Halberstrom was always doing horoscopes, but she always did them wrong. People would come over, and sit at the kitchen table and Barbara would "do their chart" and tell them what it said and charge them five dollars. Then they'd call back sooner or later and say that they had it done by a machine and she did it wrong. They she would have to do it all over again for free.

Barbara told me that I had "Leo rising" and said that I should be careful not to be too bossy because Leos could be bossy. I tried very hard never to boss Barbara, and I hoped I wasn't in any way bossing her "subconsciously," as she said I might.

She sat me down at the kitchen table one day and explained to me that I was too "fixed," which was something like being too stubborn, I think. She was wrong, though, as I later found out from going to a real astrologer, who did my chart and told me I was not fixed at all, but "mutable," and that I should watch out for being too rebellious and too flighty. She said I should be more warm-hearted and compassionate towards other people. And so I tried very hard not to be bossy and to be more warm-hearted just in case they were both right, but that hurt my feelings even though I didn't say anything just to be polite.

Barbara was always coming home with little pamphlets and fliers about different things. Barbara loved her little pamphlets and pieces of paper so much, much more than she loved anybody who was just a real person and not a piece of paper. Most of her pamphlets were about Women's Liberation, which was beginning at that time, I think.

The best pamphlet was called "No More Fun And Games."
It said that women could no longer "play the game" with
men. It hurt my feelings so much to think that men never
wanted to "play the game" with me, when I read that pamphlet. It seemed like all these women were being treated so
badly by some terrible men, but no men liked me well
enough to treat me terribly in the first place. They just
didn't seem to want to treat me any way at all, good or bad,
and the only men I knew were the Hippies Upstairs, and
they weren't regular men, it didn't seem.

Crawdaddy was the only one who ever had been mean to
me, and so I told Barbara Halberstrom about that to make
her like me more. But I don't think she cared very much. I
guess Barbara Halberstrom never liked me that much. She
said that I should be more "open" and "*live* a little bit." And
then she went off to "*live*" with some other people that she
was "more into."

I just couldn't understand why Betty Baines and Barbara
Halberstrom weren't happy living in our building with me. I
was a nice person. I didn't rob them, and I tried not to boss
them or be too cold hearted. You could do whatever you
wanted, and there was no person to order you around.
There was always someone around to smoke reefer with you
and stare into space listening to records with. You could go
out any time of the day or night, anywhere you wanted
to go.

I was very happy with my janitor work. Nobody, hardly,
ever yelled at me or made me listen to boring criticisms
about what I did. I guess things were pretty good until
Meredith Greenberg moved in.

Meredith was my next roommate. She was very happy to
live in a Yankee tenement, it seemed. This seemed pretty
funny to me especially considering that Meredith turned
out to be rich. Meredith came from a rich family, and was a
student at Radcliffe. She said lets not clean up because it's
"too, really too bourgeois."

Meredith liked being "frank" and "down to earth." She liked "facing facts." She used to tell me things that she knew. Meredith had read many books, and she knew lots of things. She even told me about where I came from. She told me that it was a "disadvantaged society." She said that The South had been disadvantaged ever since the Civil War.

That confused me because I was always told to be proud of The South and not to let the terrible uncouth Yankees bother me when I moved to The North. I wondered if Meredith was right or if I should ignore her because she was an uncouth Yankee. It *was* true that Meredith never did clean up and lived in terrible squalor. So I just told her that it was not polite to say "Civil War," and that you should say "War Between The States" instead. And then Meredith didn't know what to say to me any more.

I guess you could say Meredith was uncouth. She always read the *New York Times*, but then she would use it for "ass wipe" (as she called it). And she said we should *both* use it because it was bourgeois to spend money on toilet paper. Toilet paper was a bourgeois invention.

I didn't really understand it, but Meredith more than anything, it seemed, wanted to be poor. She half-starved herself all the time, eating only low calorie foods, and sometimes only drinking French coffee that tasted so awful and smoking French cigarettes instead of eating. Day after day I watched her, and finally I began to be ashamed of myself, eating so much every day, even *bread*. Meredith said you didn't need bread because it only turned to sugar and that was very bad for you.

I tried to look the best I could being a janitor and all, but Meredith seemed to want to look as poor as she could. She wore ragged clothes, and shoes that didn't fit and rubbed blisters on her feet. But, still, Meredith convinced ME that *I* shouldn't be so impoverished and disadvantaged and oppressed.

Meredith convinced me that I was poor, and so I went out

and got myself a little part-time job at Leaning Tower of
Pizza, so I could have more money and not be so disadvantaged. Still, I couldn't think of what it was that I ought to
be doing for myself; after all, I already had everything that I
could ever want. Wasn't I already happy? I wondered. But
Meredith said how COULD I be happy, damn it. Didn't I
know there was more to life? Didn't I? Actually, I didn't
understand that there was More To Life.

Since More To Life was what Betty Baines kept saying,
too, before she moved away, I figured I better look into this.
There wasn't any *thing* that I wanted or needed, but I
thought maybe there might be something MORE to *do*. I
decided to go to college, like everyone else. It could be
something to do.

I went to "U. Mass." It was cheap and lots of Post-War
Babies and Hippies went there. I went part-time and worked
at my janitor job and my Leaning Tower Of Pizza job
sometimes, too. I had a lot to do. I took English Grammar
and Composition, and Recent Middle Eastern History
because that was all that was left open by the time I went
over to register for my classes.

Our history teacher was a very nice man from Pakistan.
He told us about how Israel started up as a country and
about how mean the people in Israel were to the Arabs and
how the Israeli people kicked the poor Arabs out of their
own houses. That sounded terrible to me and I wondered
why I had never heard about this before. I had only heard
about the terrible persecution of the Jews, but not of
the Arabs.

I said this to Meredith that I never heard of how they took
away the houses from the Arabs, and Meredith said there
were lots of things I never heard of that they taught in
college. Colleges seemed like a very good thing to me, and I
couldn't understand why so many Hippies went around
telling people "drop out now" so much. They were always
saying that. Still, to me college seemed like a very good

thing. I wondered why Meredith Greenberg never, hardly ever went to her classes at Radcliffe. She would always just say, "Oh, God," and not answer me when I asked, but the truth was that she was only going to Radcliffe College in order to keep getting her trust fund checks.

One day I said to Meredith if she didn't like her school why didn't she let some poor person go in her place, somebody who'd *like* to go there. Meredith liked that idea, and the next semester we traded identities. I thought, of course, that it would be the greatest thing in the world to go to Radcliffe College, and Meredith thought it would be not too bad to go to U. Mass where there would be lots of poor people.

By the end of the semester, though, I had only earned Meredith a C- grade point average. Meredith was very upset because she said she would be on probation for her trust fund if she got lower than a B-. But Meredith only got a C- for me at U. Mass., too. She said that her "academic freedom" was obstructed, which "inhibited" her "performance."

I felt terrible. The other girls in my class at Radcliffe knew lots of things and had lots of beautiful clothes that they didn't even care about. They got to take ballet lessons and go on trips to Europe. I told Meredith that she was very lucky and she should appreciate what she had. She said, "Oh, God," and didn't speak to me for a little while.

When she did speak to me she told me that I was right *and* wrong, too, and we had a big talk about it. In the end Meredith said she wanted to be friends with me and have an "equal relationship." That was when Meredith started paying all the rent, to make it fair. She said it wasn't fair that I had to be a janitor AND go to school, when she could sit around and read the *New York Times* all day long if she wanted. And so she told me to make things really fair, she would pay all the rent, and I could go to college or stay home and read the *New York Times*, too, whatever I wanted.

It seemed weird, but I said thank you very much, OK.

And then I went to U. Mass full time. I took every class I
wanted to take. I found out that I liked English novels the
best. All day long I went to classes that were about English
novels or sat around and read English novels. I loved them
so much, even the long ones. I felt so happy.

Meredith wasn't happy, still, at all. She said our lives were
"stagnating," and it was time for her to move on. She moved
on to Paris and I went back to being a janitor. Still, I kept
taking my classes about English novels and reading a lot. It
made me happy. But I got so spoiled by not working when
Meredith Greenberg was paying the rent that I hated my
janitor job and I started getting depressed.

Slowly I began to feel kind of crummy, just like most
everyone else around me seemed to feel sooner or later.
Slowly I began to understand why so many other people
seemed to feel so bad so much. Slowly it began to occur to
me that maybe life was not, after all, even worth the trouble.
Here I was, young and "free" and in The World. And it was
all crummy. Nobody had appeared to open the Magical
Doors Of Happiness. They only opened for Meredith
Greenberg, who had a secret key. For me, the doors were all
locked. The future was all locked. I had no secret key, no
free pass; but Meredith could go through even though she
didn't want to. I could see that all I was gonna be able to do
in life was sit in the servants quarters and read a book. Yes,
there was more to life, but not for me.

I got depressed and gave up. Everything was bleak. Mrs.
Potter just seemed dumb. Barbara Halberstrom seemed
silly. Betty Baines was long gone, and Meredith Greenberg
was in some fancy place in Paris. All I got was more stuff to
clean and more Great Books Of The Western World taught
by married ladies from the suburbs.

I found that giving up was easy once I had given up. All
you have to do is give up when you give up. You just sit back
and give up. I slept whenever possible, and spoke only when
it was absolutely necessary. I did my janitor job as slowly as

possible and dropped out of U. Mass. The Hippies upstairs
said, "great, man, far out."

The Hippies told me that I was making progress. They
said if I would just "get off my bummer," I'd see how
beautiful life could be now that I was free. To start me off on
the rest of my new life, they gave me a capsule of LSD, which
they had all taken. I felt like I had nothing to lose, and so I
swallowed it. In about twenty minutes I began to feel nervous. Hyperventilating, I got dizzy and began to feel sick to
my stomach. When I finally began to vomit I could see all the
colorful little particles of throw-up swirling and dancing
magically in the toilet bowl. I stared into the toilet in wonder, but I could not stop vomiting.

When my little blood vessels could no longer endure the
strain of the heaving, I began to vomit blood. Watching the
colors change, I wondered if the color red was "real." To
help out, my "friends" gave me another pill, a valium, and
told me to lie down that I'd feel better soon. It was just a "bad
trip" they said, and then they went away to do something
groovy, and went off and left me.

I did lie down, and was soon unable to move at all.
Nothing, no part of me could move—except the little finger
on my right hand. That was all I could move. I didn't know if
I were dying or getting paralyzed or if I were just very
depressed, but I couldn't move at all. For the next seven and
a half hours I remained motionless except for one small
finger, which I tried to exercise to make sure I was still alive.

About half way through my "trip" I did think I was going
to die. My life swirled in front of me, as I lay dying on that
very mattress on that very floor in that very Yankee Tenement apartment. My life passed all around me, scene after
scene floating by in spirals, like a piece of video tape that had
fallen out of its little can undeveloped. I said good-bye to
it all, and prepared myself for the here-after when the
doorbell rang.

I let the bell ring and ring, dying as I was, motionless as I was. How could I answer the doorbell? I lay there and thought about how I could answer it. I wondered how to answer it without moving, but I couldn't come up with an idea. Finally this woman just walked in. "Hello! Your door is open! Is anybody here?" she called. I called back, whispering, "hellllo . . ." Then she said "Hello? Hello?" And I said back feebly in my whisper, my dying death whisper, "Hellllo . . . . hellllo . . ."

It was Jocelyn. She kept calling back confidently, "Hello? Hello?," following my voice until she got to the bedroom where I lay dying on the floor. Jocelyn gasped:

"My God, are *you* the cleaning woman?"

"Yes, I ammmm . . . . ."

"Are you allright?"

"Yessssssss. I'mmmmm fiiiiinnnnne."

"Well, you don't *look* fine! Are you the one that left an ad in the paper for doing house cleaning?"

"Yesssss. Just leave your nnnnnaaaame and phone nnnnnummmmmmmmber on a piece of paper . . . ."

At this point, although I had put ads in several papers saying "cleaning lady available," I went back to dying, with which I had been very busy before being interrupted. From that moment until my LSD wore off, Jocelyn sat there and held my little finger. At some point my "friends" came back from grooving around the neighborhood and told Jocelyn what happened. She told them get the fuck out of her sight, how could they just leave somebody in that kind of condition all alone. She wanted to call an ambulance, but they talked her out of that. I was glad because I sure didn't want to die in an ambulance.

But, anyway, that LSD did wear off after some hours went by, and Jocelyn did sit there and hold my finger the whole time. I never forgot that. I never did manage to die that time. I don't know why not; I was all ready to go and everything.

About a week later I moved into Jocelyn's apartment to be

her live-in baby-sitter. Since that time I have always felt that
Jocelyn saved my life. I do believe that Jocelyn saved my life;
but Jocelyn said that I wouldn't have died even if she hadn't
come in, that maybe I would have gone crazy or something
like that or passed out or something. But I *know* that I was (as
they said in Phoebus) "fixin' to die." Jocelyn, I had no doubt,
saved my life, and from that time on I owed her mine.

Life in Roxbury, a Black Area
With a Few White People

JOCELYN WAS WHITE, and she had a daughter who was Black, and that's why Jocelyn was living in Roxbury. Roxbury was the Black part of town, and Jocelyn lived there so that MiMi, her Black daughter, could fit into the environment better.

Even though MiMi was actually a tan color, like a Hawaiian, Jocelyn said that she would be called "Black" by everybody. Jocelyn figured that since she was the one who was grown-up, and not MiMi, that it was only fair that she herself be the outcast one of a neighborhood, the one who would be hated and a misfit, instead of her little baby girl. Sad to say, but most every neighborhood is very hateful and racist in Boston. Like lots of places.

I thought that Jocelyn and MiMi should, actually, go and live in Hawaii for a long time until I found out that in Hawaii they have terrible racism, too, and that the tan-skinned people call the white-skinned people "howlies" or something, and that the White people are mean to everyone else, just like they are mostly everywhere.

Anyway, MiMi was a great color of golden tan, and she had hair that was that color, too. All golden. Her hair sprung out from her head in cute little golden springy wisps. It was cute.

Although Jocelyn had a daughter of the opposite race, there was not much of anything else that was weird about her, except that she was braver than most people, and you could say she had a "bigger mouth."

You could say that Jocelyn, in fact, was a "straight person," as the Hippies would say. She never did drugs or had sex with strangers, well, almost never. And she also had a "straight job" at a big university in the personnel department. That's how she met "Gem," MiMi's father.

Gem was friends with a guy that Jocelyn liked. Jocelyn was trying to get the Hiring Committee to hire this guy for a certain job even though everybody said how the guy was a "job hopper." Jocelyn managed to convince the Hiring Committee, though, that this guy had only been a "hopper" because he hadn't been able to find any job that suited him yet, and that it wasn't his fault.

Gem was a graduate student and a teaching assistant at that same school. It turned out that the "hopper," Gem, and Jocelyn all got to be good friends, as Jocelyn told me, and that they had a really great time. Then, Jocelyn told me, she and Gem fell in love and moved in together, and she got pregnant, and they had a baby.

Then, she said, the "hopper" did, after all, quit his job that Jocelyn fought so hard to get him; and Gem started getting into the habit of "experimenting" with drugs. Then, Jocelyn said, that Gem said that these drugs made him "see more clearly." And then Jocelyn said that Gem said that he "saw" that he wasn't "into" living with Jocelyn and/or MiMi anymore after a while, and so he moved out.

After Gem moved out, Jocelyn said, he started doing

drugs all the time, and quit coming over any more. He just paid MiMi a stupid little visit once in a while, Jocelyn said, and never paid any child support ever at all.

It seemed that Jocelyn would never forgive Gem for doing that. It was for MiMi's sake that she didn't forgive him. I used to tell Jocelyn that she should forgive Gem for it so that she wouldn't have to live with hate in her heart, but Jocelyn disagreed and said he could not be forgiven because he was an asshole and then I said couldn't she just forgive him for selfish reasons but she said, "that asshole? You have got to be kidding."

Sometimes Jocelyn would take MiMi to Philadelphia to visit Gem's relatives, partly because they were nice people, and partly so MiMi could get to know her Black kin, Jocelyn said. The relatives in Philadelphia got to know MiMi and Jocelyn pretty well after a while and they told her that they felt closer to her and MiMi than they did to Gem because Gem never came to visit them any more, either.

Gem's relatives still to this day get along very well with Jocelyn and MiMi, but they like to remind Jocelyn, just as a joke, I guess, that she "wasted her Whiteness." They said, Jocelyn said, that Whiteness was worth good money, and Jocelyn went and squandered hers on Gem.

Anyway, Jocelyn decided to stay in Roxbury and waste her Whiteness there. Jocelyn did this all really deliberately. She used to think about it and talk about it all the time. But I just arrived in Roxbury by accident, and if I hadn't been dying on my acid trip that day, I might not ever have lived there at all.

You could say that Jocelyn "took me in," like a wet puppy or something. I guess that's why the large dog in the sleet at the bus stop that night has upset me for such a long time. I knew how bad it must have felt, how awful it felt; but I didn't rescue it, even though Jocelyn rescued me and I was OK again.

I was on my way back home to Jocelyn's one night as

usual. It was February in Boston and turning colder, just at that time of year when the worst winter weather was happening. It wasn't raining or snowing that night, but it was sleeting.

Half-soaked and half-frozen, like everything else, a dog appeared at the bus stop. It was a large city-colored dog, a grayish and semi-invisible beige color, actually no particular color, but you could tell it by its big round, begging eyes. It looked at me with a look of hope, very politely, as we waited for the bus.

If it had been a person there with me that night, it might have robbed me; but it was just a polite, large, hopeful and colorless dog. We waited together for the bus. When the bus arrived, however, I got on, and left the dog in the dark, cold and homeless in the winter night, in the sleet. Almost midnight. No one else around and not another bus for an hour. In another hour it might have died of the cold, but I hope to the Lord that it found some place to go hide.

Of all the sins, of omission or commission, that I have ever committed or ommitted, that sin stays with me, haunting me always year after year. And crazy though it might seem to you, when that memory comes back to me I wish to heaven that I could go back and get that dog, and love it, and keep it, and be its friend, and sacrifice my whole life for it, even. If only I could do that now, go back and get it. If only I had warmed it up, given it a home. But I didn't.

Of course, I didn't WANT to let that dog stay out and freeze itself in the sleet. I wanted to take it back to Jocelyn's. The trouble was that I didn't even have a home for myself really at the time, let alone for a large, wet, colorless and very polite dog. At that time I only had Jocelyn's home to stay in, and Jocelyn hated dogs. She really hated them. I don't know why, but she said that there wasn't even enough to go around for the poor people of the world, never mind dogs and cats. But one day Jocelyn did get a cat anyway.

Of course, I didn't want to leave it. I wish I had kept it, but

I didn't. I failed my spiritual mission, flunked my exam. I seem to flunk my spiritual tests over and over. That is how it seems to me, but Jocelyn says that this is not true. She says that I'm a "rescuer," and one thing about a being rescuer is that you never get to rescue anyone, you never do save anyone hardly, you just stick with them and practically drown yourself with them. I have learned that about myself, and I guess Jocelyn has that thing in her, too, only more.

Anyway, Jocelyn did pretty much rescue me, and I didn't bring that dog back to her house cause I didn't want to get her all mad and everything. So I stayed at Jocelyn's for a pretty long time, and after I'd been there about six months or so I started feeling better and better, just about as good as I used to feel in the old days before I ever met Meredith Greenberg.

I gained some weight at Jocelyn's and Jocelyn lost some weight after I came so that we could wear each other's clothes. That was lots of fun because Jocelyn had lots of sexy things with low necklines and stuff that I never had. And Jocelyn thought it was fun, too, even though I had crummy stuff, it was all in skinny sizes that Jocelyn never thought she would be able to fit into. So Jocelyn felt happy in my old skinny jeans and tee-shirts, and I felt happy in her low-cut blouses, even though I was a little bit more flat-chested than Jocelyn was.

Jocelyn wasn't flat chested in the least, and men were always staring at her bosom. One day we went with some neighbors to a local bar (they call them bar-rooms in Boston). This man kept staring at Jocelyn's bosom over and over.

Finally Jocelyn got sick of it, and since she was wearing a summer sun-dress and since it was easy to do, she just pulled her whole top of her dress right down over her bosom for everyone to see. Then she pulled her dress up again real fast and that guy was so shocked that he didn't stare at her bosom any more at all. In fact, he got out of there very fast.

We had lots of friendly neighbors in Roxbury, it turned

out. They weren't hateful at all, even though we were White. We had cook-outs in the back yard. And MiMi got more and more beautiful all the time. It was like having little Peggy back again but a couple years older. I was so happy. Sometimes Mrs. Potter would even come over and we'd all watch TV together. It was fun.

After a while I went back to U. Mass. again. I got some scholarship money. I took care of MiMi in the mornings and Mrs. Potter took care of her in the afternoons. Jocelyn took care of her at nights. It all worked out.

Jocelyn had an entire huge second floor flat, and she paid less for it than I paid for my own one room in my Yankee Tenement apartment over in Cambridge where all the Post War Babies lived. At Jocelyn's, too, we did all the normal things that the people in Cambridge never seemed to do: we shopped for bargains at the grocery store, we baked apple pies, and we even washed the floors in the corners. Jocelyn had a dining room table and two sets of china even, and we even had Sunday dinners like back in Phoebus and invited the neighbors over. I liked it.

It was pretty normal there at Jocelyn's. There was no man there, but there was everything else normal like regular families had. It was pretty, too. Most people think if you live in a "ghetto" that it's going to be all rundown and shabby. But Jocelyn's apartment was in a beautiful old Victorian house, just the kind that all the rich people want to take over nowadays. It was in perfect repair and there was even a little rose garden. It was so beautiful. We even hung our sheets out to dry and nobody stole them and it made them smell so nice and fresh. I guess most people don't care if their sheets smell fresh, but it smells so good like that. Meredith Greenberg would just say it was bourgeois or something.

The kind of bad thing about Jocelyn's apartment was that it was painted all gray. The walls and even the floors and everything were all gray. I guess some people would think that was real chic, but it wasn't. It was ugly and made people feel depressed. The neighbors would ask me a lot how come it was all gray in there. Jocelyn told me it was because she got the gray paint for cheap, but I knew it was because Gem moved out and Jocelyn felt so sad and angry and gray-like in her mind.

One day Jocelyn decided to paint her walls over again. She said she would go ahead and "spend the money." This time she got hot pink and turquoise, and lawn green. It was a bad mistake. "Oh, God, oh shit," she said. She had to paint all over again. "I have no imagination," Jocelyn said. But it wasn't true. Jocelyn just had *too good* of an imagination. I said why didn't she just paint all the walls white like they did in Cambridge, but she said that would be too boring.

In the end, she left some walls turquoise or lawn green, and turned some walls back to gray. It was kind of neat, and everybody said how did she get it to look so good. I don't know how Jocelyn did get it to look so good, but Jocelyn said you could have odd things in your life, but you had to have them in the right combination. Anyway, Jocelyn quit painting then and went on about her business of having affairs with married men. She liked it.

Pretty soon Jocelyn was having a good old time, and things were looking up. Still, even though things were looking up, I started getting depressed again. I started having that same old feeling that there must be More To Life, just like Betty Baines and Meredith Greenberg used to say.

I didn't have any boyfriend, and nothing special was going on . . . well, except for the Viet Nam War, and terrible things. Special things like *that* seemed to be happening all the time, bomb alarms at U. Mass. and "trashing" the streets and all kinds of things, but no *good* special things too much.

At U. Mass. the Post War Babies were busy thinking of things to do to protest about the Viet Nam War. They had rallies and marches and they lay down in the streets getting arrested in front of big trucks and stuff.

One day I went to a meeting. Everybody was busy think-

ing of what could they do about the War in Viet Nam, and
somebody said, "Well, that's what you get with capitalism."
That person said that what you have to do is organize the
workers. He said did anyone live in a big apartment in a
"working class" neighborhood. I said I did, and he said
would it be all right to have a party there and I could invite
all my neighbors and we would tell everyone about the Viet
Nam War and have them to sign a petition.

I asked Jocelyn if we could have a party and invite all the
neighbors to come and sign a petition. She said sure, she
didn't care as long as she didn't have to clean up afterwards.

That evening all the neighbors came over. All the socialists came over. We had a big party, and the neighbors signed
the petition and the socialists all talked about the War in Viet
Nam and the Ruling Class and everything and they made
me very mad. They didn't care about us or the neighbors at
all, and in the end they just went away and left a big mess and
I had to clean up.

The neighbors stayed, though. They said I shouldn't be
mad at the college students because they were just young
and they didn't know what they were talking about. The
neighbors said why was I still mad anyway, all the college
students left early. They said it was just some college student
communists and what did it matter they were gone. But I
was still mad after the college student communists left. I was
jealous. It was because they kept talking about the workers
all the time, and most of them didn't have to go to work. I
did. That made me so mad.

The next day I was still mad. Jocelyn said she never saw
me get so mad before. I hated them, it was true, and I didn't
even know them. Jocelyn said, "Why don't you do something REAL, something that could really help the struggle
against the War in Viet Nam instead of listening to a bunch
of lefty windbags." And so I went around our neighborhood by myself with my own petition and asked even more
of the neighbors to sign up and register to vote. They said
they would.

The neighbors looked at me kind of funny, the ones I didn't know. I guess it was because I was White but maybe it was because I was funny-looking and skinny. And when I turned my petition into the petition office, I didn't feel like I had done anything REAL at all, not at all. I felt like I just wasted my time. Then one day I walked into a poster store, just looking around. There was a poster that had a picture of a Black woman who lived in the old days, and underneath the picture it said, "More Dangerous Than A Thousand Rioters." It was about Lucy Parsons, an agitator. And there was a quote at the bottom of the poster, something she said at a meeting of workers. It said:

> Send forth your petition, and let them read it by the red glare of destruction. You can be assured that you have spoken to the robbers in the only language which they have ever been able to understand.

I didn't understand it, really, but it made me feel better after I wasted my time sending petitions to Richard Nixon that there was somebody else who felt like sending out petitions was a waste of time, too.

I kept thinking of what I could do to end the War In Viet Nam. Jocelyn never thought of what could she do to end the War In Viet Nam. She said she had enough to do having a baby by herself. So I went back to Cambridge to the old apartment where I used to live and talked to The Hippies Upstairs.

They said you just have to stop the soldiers from going over there to fight and then there wouldn't be a war because they wouldn't have anyone to fight in it. Of course, some men didn't go to The War. They went to Canada or some other foreign country or even to jail.

I felt sorry the most for the men who went to jail. I decided to do some volunteer work for the Draft Counselling enter in Cambridge. I wanted to help people (guys) find ways to get out of the Army. So I went over to the place and there was just this one guy there, and I told him I wanted to help out and he said well, what could you do? And I said I could answer the phone and read up on what people were doing and look things up in books and get lots of plans and ideas or else I could wash the floor or paint the walls or file papers or make sandwiches or anything there was to do.

But the guy in the office said no, I could not work there because even if I worked for free it wouldn't do them any good because I wasn't a man and I couldn't possibly know everything that men knew about getting drafted and that I just wouldn't be able to understand. So I went away.

I went back to the Hippie Apartment and told them what happened at the Draft Counselling Center. I said what else could I do to help end The War In View Nam? Me and this guy, Zoom, talked and talked. We thought and thought. We figured we could go to the place where all the guys went to get on the bus to go to where they were going to be "inducted." It seemed like the last chance to talk to somebody before they went in the Army.

Zoom and I found out that there was this one place where they were going to be loading guys up on buses to take them to the Army and that they were going to be loading them up there at this place the next morning at 5:30 a.m. It turned out that lots of other people had the same idea, and that lots of people were going to be there giving out leaflets and cookies and everything. Zoom and I decided to make some cookies for them.

We went to the grocery store and got everything we needed to make oatmeal raisin cookies. We got back, and Zoom turned on the oven and I got all the stuff all measured out. Then Zoom just stopped. He said, "this is a waste of time. They'll just eat all our cookies for breakfast, and take our leaflet and throw it away without even reading it or listening to us." I said that we could talk very fast and make them think about what they were doing before they could finish eating them.

Zoom said, "yeah, sure." And then he stopped dead still

and looked at me. "Shit," he said, "we'd have to put something pretty damn good into those fucking cookies to make anybody stop and listen and think THAT much." Zoom looked at me. I looked at him.

Zoom said, "what's colorless, odorless, and tasteless?"

We ran to the freezer where Zoom had stashed his LSD. We got it out and unfroze it. It was straight from the lab, Zoom said. We never did make any cookies. We decided that it wasn't fair to make somebody take LSD if they didn't decide on their own that they wanted to. We thought that it was kind of like sending people to the Army no matter if they wanted to go or not, and so we took some LSD ourselves and spent a very long time thinking if there was anything else we could do to stop people from going into the Army.

We couldn't think of anything. But I was glad that I took the LSD because I could see that it could be a wonderful experience. I did not die or vomit or anything this time. After a while we forgot about the Viet Nam War. We went for a walk outside. It was a beautiful October day. All the leaves were red and gold or dead. They were all over the sidewalk, and if you kicked them, you could see their light rays all over the place streaming into the street and onto your foot. It was wonderful to see so many light rays, and so much beauty that I had not stopped to admire and appreciate. There was a little kid playing with a red ball in the street. It was such a beautiful ball. It rolled so perfectly smoothly. It was so round and red, you could see the light rays bouncing off of it. I could feel the wind in my hair.

Taking LSD gave me a new lease on life. I decided to make every day a celebration. That lasted about two weeks before I got depressed again. I still didn't have a boyfriend, and nothing was special. The View Nam War went on, and on. Every night on the TV news you could see people getting blown up in Viet Nam. It was awful, and I couldn't think of anything to do about it, it was just like being a helpless slave, sitting there watching people getting blown up in Viet Nam. It was very depressing if you thought about it.

I just had to stop thinking about it, I decided, if there wasn't anything I could do. I thought about falling in love instead. After all, I had nobody to be my boyfriend and I was getting to be a woman. Some people even said I already was a woman, although I noticed that people called women "girls" even when they were forty or fifty.

Before I left Phoebus Mom warned me, "You're getting to be a woman now. You're going to have to start looking like one." I remembered that. It was a warning and a threat, an omen and a portent of a dreadful punishment that was going to befall me: I was going to be a woman, and there was nothing I could do to stop it.

I thought about that, and it was a terrifying thought. It was a true thought, though, I thought; and so it might also be true that I was going to have to start looking like one. Probably Mom was right. Mom said it wasn't so hard to look like a woman. All you needed was a little lipstick and the right clothes and roll up your hair.

I looked in the mirror and decided to look like a woman. Since it was the new times, you didn't need to roll up your hair, and everybody just wore their jeans or their little short skirts; that wasn't too hard. It seemed like all I needed to do was get some make-up. I was too plain. There was nothing at all special about me, and so it figured that nothing special was happening to me in my life. I wanted to look special.

I got some white lipstick and some eye make-up, just like the Hippies did. It seemed to me that the Hippie Girls all looked very special. Some Hippie girls said you should look natural and not wear any make-up, but they didn't look special to me. But other Hippie Girls wore lots and lots of eye-liner and eye-shadow. I liked that.

I bought lots of eye make-up. It was beautiful. I wore lots of it, layers of Sea Green and Misty Lavender. Splotches of Purple Ice. I felt beautiful. I would have preferred ballet shoes and trips to Europe to feel special and beautiful, but this was all I could afford. Still, I didn't fall in love.

I knew that being in love was the only thing that would make my life special. I wanted to fall in love so much. But I did not fall in love. I waited and waited. But I did not fall in love. The War In Viet Nam went on and on. I watched it every night on TV. It was awful, and I could not think about it any more because I still could not think of any way to stop it. I went to some demonstrations. That did not work. It went on and on.

Once again I began to give up and get depressed. This time I found a new way to give up: by listening to music. I had lots of old records that I loved very much. I listened to them over and over, sitting there staring into space all alone. Jocelyn didn't like my old records. It didn't seem that any-one else liked my old records but me. I had saved them from the old days at Billy's Bar-B-Que when Betty Baines and I would practice our dance steps.

My favorite songs were: "Gotta Make a Come-back to Your Heart," by Eddie Floyd, and "Lover's Prayer," by Otis Redding. It was a wonderful song. I played it about 50,000 times. But I loved, still, the songs that not so many people liked. The kinds of songs I liked were called "Do Wop" songs, but most of the people my age liked "psychedelic" music and not "Do Wop." I don't know why, but the people I liked best never got to be very popular: Hughie Hughes and the Hugos, Dreama Darlene and the Darlings, and The Ricochets. But my number one favorite of all was by The Shepards. It was called *Island of Love*. I wanted to go, go, go, as the lyrics said. I wanted to go, go, go. I wanted, also to "drown in a sea of love," which they were always singing about in my songs, too.

I hated White people's music. The best Do Wop songs were by Black groups and individuals. It seemed to me that they could sing the best by far, and I hated listening to all those terrible screechy noises in psychedelic music. I also hated Easy Listenin and Annette Funicello and all of those songs, too. I hated "Itsy bitsy teeny weeny yellow polka dot bikini." I wanted to drown in a sea of love after having visited the Island of Love, where I always, always wanted to go, go, go. It never stopped inside me, this sick, romantic notion of suicide.

I began to wonder, in fact, what it felt like to drown, actually drown. It seemed like such a wonderful thing to do, to go to a deserted beach on a beautiful day and walk into the water and never come back. I never did it, though, drown. Although I did take some scuba diving lessons at the YMCA, but Jocelyn knew what was going on in my mind, and she said cut it out that this was the most complicated suicide plot in town and just stop it right now. I said how did she know what I was thinking anyway and she said it was because she could tell I hated scuba diving lessons that it seemed to make me miserable on my days when I went to the pool at the YMCA.

So I stopped my scuba diving lessons and continued listening to my Do Wop records all alone:

> Starry night, the moon is bright,
> I want you to come to me.
> Somewhere in the night
> I should be holding you tight . . . (etc.)

It was a big surprise when a likely candidate showed up. His name was Bipsy Street, and he was a musician. Bipsy Street lived on the edge of Roxbury but he wasn't Black; he was White. Still, he played in a Black club near our house, the Candlelight Lounge.

Me and Jocelyn and some of our friends from our neighborhood used to go to the Candlelight Lounge on the weekends and Bipsy Street and The Bops sometimes played there. Bipsy Street always played Do Wop music. He knew just how to do it even though he was White. He was a drummer, and he always got the rhythm just right. It was a dream come true.

When I'd see him at the Candlelight Lounge, he would be all dressed up and fancy looking. Usually he'd wear white shoes, a purple suit, a black tie, and a pink shirt. Then when he'd get hot from playing his drums he'd take off his pink shirt and his black neck tie and play his drums in his old white undershirt and it was very exciting. It was easy for me and Bipsy to notice each other because we would pretty much be the only White people at the Candlelight Lounge except for Jocelyn, who would come in with one of her married men.

I suppose that Bipsy and I could have had a fine romance, I suppose that we DID have a fine romance, despite the fact that Bipsy was married. Bipsy's wife, Dalia, was always great to me, though, and invited me over to dinner and everything at least once a week.

I never did understand what kind of relationship Bipsy and I had, and why Dalia wasn't jealous of me (not that she had much of a reason to be jealous of ME except that I was "getting it on" with her husband). I was in love with her husband, though, and he did seem to like me pretty well, too. In fact, I can say that I did love her husband, and he did love me, but still there wasn't much of a reason to be jealous of me, and I guess that's why she didn't seem to get bothered by me.

Almost all Bipsy and I would do was sit around and make up Do Wop songs together, and make up dance steps, and try to sing in harmony (which I could not do very well). Bipsy made up very good classical do wop songs:

> Please be honest from the start,
> I've been hurt, sweetheart.
> Don't let it happen – AGAIN.
>
> If I give my love to you,
> will you promise to be true.
> Don't let it happen AGAIN . . . (etc.)

We never got tired of it and I guess Dalia just got bored and sick of us sitting around their living room making up dumb songs. But we didn't get sick of it at all. Sometimes I would make up the lyrics and Bipsy would write down the music to it. My best one was called "Red Hot Mamma," although as more like blues and not classical Do Wop:

> I'm a red hot mamma, I got nothing to say,
> I'm too hot to handle. I give off infra red rays.
> I've been to 400 cities, had 800 men,
> and I'll get to you, too, child, but I don't know when.
> You see I'm busy at the moment, I got a job in a lion's den,
> but I'll get to you, honey, just as soon as I can . . . (etc.)

It was a good song, but nobody but me and Bipsy ever liked it. Another great one that I made up was a psychedelic rock and roll song. It was called "Prophylactic Man":

> I always get the best, I get the 4-× brand.
> My baby, she calls me "Prophylactic Man". . . (etc.)

It was very stupid, but some Hippies liked it, and Bipsy ended up getting into a band with a bunch of White people and they played it and a bunch of other psychedelic songs and they got to be more and more famous. I didn't get to see Bipsy so much after that, but when I did it was still special.

One day Bipsy, Dalia, and I were sitting around. I was thinking how great Bipsy and Dalia were to me, and about how we all cared so very deeply about each other. Dalia said she knew how much we all cared about each other, and she knew how much Bipsy and I cared about each other, and maybe it would be nice if I moved in. I said I would love that more than anything in the world, but I didn't feel right about me and Bipsy caring so much about each other and being alone sometimes without her. I said it didn't seem right.

We all got drunk together that night, and went and got in Bipsy and Dalia's big bed. Well, actually Bipsy and I got drunk and Dalia just went to bed with us sober. We all had sex together you could say, all three of us in bed there at the same time.

But it was a big confusion of arms, legs, and things, none of which seemed to me to belong to any particular person. It all kind of seemed like everything belonged to everybody, to ALL of us, as if all the arms and legs and flesh and things were part of everyone. Still, it did not seem very sexy to me, and it did not work out very well in the end, I guess, because Bipsy and Dalia never called me back again after that; I don't know why. I hope I didn't do anything to hurt their feelings. I never did find out what was wrong. I suppose this kind of thing is sometimes called an "orgy," but back in the sixties everyone just said "that's far out" when anyone talked about something like that. I don't know.

Studying Astrology

ONE DAY I bought myself a copy of the *A to Z Horoscope Maker and Delineator,* and I taught myself how to do horoscopes—just to see what it was like. I got pretty good at it, and made fewer mistakes than Barbara Halberstrom, which isn't saying much. Even though I am not very smart or very well educated at all, I learned astrology pretty easily.

I started talking to Barbara Halberstrom about astrology and she said that I was learning it very fast. She said I learned it fast because even though I am not very smart necessarily or very well educated, I can think abstractly. That's how she explained it. But I just love astrology so much because it gives you a special language to use for thinking and talking about invisible (but still alive) vibrations.

Some people still do not know this, but vibrations are real things, and astrology can give you a time table to let you know when certain invisible vibrations can be passing over you or growing inside you. There are even some concrete, scientific reasons why this could be true, but I don't understand them, because I cannot pay attention when people talk about these things, and so I do not know about them. But there are some reasons.

I don't know why astrology "works" but it does work and it is real and true, if you can understand that the real and true vibrations will come around to you and will grow inside you, but you may not get an "event" to make it seem "real" to you just because the real vibration is there. But lots of times you truly get an event as well as the vibration, but the vibration doesn't HAVE to become "concrete," that's all. That's what I think anyway.

One day I decided to have my horoscope ("chart") done by a famous astrologer. I called up Alice Millardi. Alice Millardi had written lots of books about astrology and she was very famous. The trouble with seeing Alice Millardi was that she lived way out in the suburbs and you had to have a car to get there. So she said to me why didn't I go see her good friend, Mildred McKenzie. Alice Millardi said that Mildred McKenzie lived right in Boston in Back Bay, and that she was a "top-notch" astrologer. I did take that advice, and called her up.

Mildred McKenzie lived, it was true, in Back Bay in Boston. It was easy to get there on the MTA. The first two times I went to see Mildred McKenzie, though, she wasn't there. She forgot that I was coming over and wasn't home. But finally, the third time I went there she was home and I had my "reading."

Mildred McKenzie was rich, you could tell. She lived in a big apartment with lots of rooms. In the front of the apartment there was a kind of small bookstore, but it was private and you had to be a member and make an appointment in order to look at the books. I asked Mildred McKenzie how come it was private, and she said that they were special books of interest only to the "initiated." I said, "Oh."

Then she took me to the back of the apartment, past the

room where Mr. McKenzie was taking a nap, she said, and past the room where she had yoga and meditation group meetings. It was very quiet in Mildred McKenzie's apartment, and it smelled like jasmine. It was very lovely, and there were pictures of Buddhas and angels and things. I liked it. I wondered if Mr. McKenzie liked all of this, too, or whether he and Mildred McKenzie had lots of fights, but it was none of my business.

Mildred McKenzie seemed to be a very nervous person, and maybe she needed all of this stuff to calm herself down, all the angels and yoga and everything—for her nerves. She tried to be calm, though:

"Come in, my dear, sit down, sit down."

"Thank you," I said, "thank you."

"Well, I see you're going to be getting married soon?"

"No," I said, "not that I know of."

"No?, Well, it says here that you'll get married very soon, within six months. Of course, these things can happen very suddenly, you know, last minute and everything. Oh, well, of course, it will be just one of those things. You'll be the one. You'll just say that you've had enough. It will last about a year and a half."

This wasn't the kind of reading that I wanted. And it wasn't the kind of a reading that I expected, either. It was very upsetting to hear that I would be getting divorced when I wasn't even married (yet). Mildred McKenzie said I was a very "rebellious young woman," but I wanted to tell Mildred McKenzie that I was not either a rebellious young woman, and that I would never do such a terrible thing as to marry someone and then break my promise and divorce him. I wanted to tell Mildred McKenzie that I tried to be good, but I didn't tell her anything. I just sat and listened.

On my way back home to Jocelyn's I felt pretty spaced out. I thought of everyone I knew, and it didn't seem that anybody I knew wanted to get married at all, except for Betty Baines and Bipsy Street and Dalia, and I never saw them any more. Nobody wanted to marry *me* anyway, that was for sure.

When I got back to Jocelyn's I told her about my reading. I was still weirded out, but when I told Jocelyn she didn't get weirded out in the least. She just said, "Oh, you just liked it because she told you that you were going to get married." But I didn't really like it exactly. Jocelyn didn't get it. Jocelyn did concrete thinking, and did not understand invisible vibrations.

In a way, I did like my reading, but in a way, I didn't. On the good side, maybe I would fall in love. On the bad side, it didn't seem like it would work out too well. I didn't know what to think.

I started studying astrology more and more. I couldn't get Mildred McKenzie's reading out of my mind. I studied and studied so that I could find out why Mildred McKenzie had said those things to me. I knew that I could not be the kind of person who would get divorced. It was very hard to believe that.

But the more I studied my horoscope, the more I began to see that maybe I was the kind of person who would get divorced, and that I was, too, a very rebellious girl.

But the more I reconsidered the whole thing, the more I knew I could never be the kind of person who would too get a divorce, and so I just figured that I must have had the wrong time of birth, and so my horoscope must just be based on incorrect data. The correct horoscope for the incorrect time.

I tried hard to find my real and truly correct birth time, but Mom and my birth certificate still said "11:47 p.m." After checking with them the only thing I could figure out was that the clock in the maternity department must have been wrong, and there was nothing I could do about it if the clock in the maternity department of the hospital where I was born was wrong. Since I could not find out my true and real time of birth, I had to give up on my horoscope.

Pretty soon I started getting depressed again without my astrology to keep me going. I started watching TV. I watched it for hours at a time. Channel 2. Channel 56. Channel 4. Every channel. I knew the program schedules by heart.

On Saturday mornings I watched cartoons with MiMi. I didn't like cartoons, and MiMi didn't like them either, but we watched anyway. MiMi always got scared, and sat in terror. There was always a small bird or mouse being smashed by a wicked coyote or bear. Sometimes a cat or a vulture would get exploded in its own TNT that it was saving for another creature, and sometimes a fox or a dog would get catapulted off a cliff. And there was always some stupid lady mouse in a tight dress who got rescued from a terrible ogre, and a polka-dotted lizard who was always saying, "Hey, kids, eat Jungle Berries, and grow up big and strong like me!"

One Saturday morning, Meredith Greenberg called up and said that she was back from Paris. She said that she met Barbara Halberstrom at a party the night before, and that Barbara Halberstrom told her that I did very good horoscopes now, and would I please look up the horoscope of that day and tell her if it were a good day because there was going to be another party that afternoon and she was tired but should she go anyway and did I want to go, too. I said that I would look up the day and call her back.

I looked up the day. Yes, it was going to be a very good day in the stars, a very good day to go to a party, an excellent day. I called Meredith Greenberg back and told her everything looked good and she said did I want to go and I said no, I was "into" cartoons all morning and old movies on TV during the afternoon. Then she said that I could come late in the afternoon after the old movies on TV, but I said no, I would be watching Jackpot Bowling late in the afternoon. Meredith Greenberg said I must be crazy and we hung up the phone.

I went back to watching Mighty Mouse and Sylvester and Tweetie Bird, and all the other little TV animals killing each other with frying pans and being run over by trains or pushed off cliffs.

When the old movies started coming on, I thought of Mrs. Potter. I thought of how she always pushed me out the door and said I was an Old Lady. She was right. Mrs. Potter would have gone to the party in a minute. Meredith said there would be musicians there at that party from all over the world, and that she met this one musician from Paris when she was there and he was very nice and everything. I thought about it some more.

I double-checked the planetary positions for the day. It was, actually, even a better day than I thought it was going to be at first glance. March sixth, season of Pisces, sign of mystical cosmic love, divine compassion, and music. A "Grand Trine" would be in effect just at 4:00, by coincidence, just as the party was supposed to be starting.

A "grand trine" means that three planets are all an equal distance from each other, and that is very good. Venus (goddess of beauty and personal love) would be equidistant from Neptune (ruler of cosmic love), and both Venus and Neptune would both be equidistant from Jupiter (the jovial planet of optimism and expansiveness). A Grand Trine. Very unusual. The afternoon, according to my books, would be a time of spiritual love, and anyone listening to beautiful music at this time would certainly experience this beautiful, invisible vibration. I called Meredith Greenberg back.

I told Meredith that I would meet her at the Hancock Bar and Grill at 3:00. Yes, I told her, it was a good day to listen to music. By 2:00 I was out of the house, and happily on my way to the MTA stop to go over to Cambridge.

It was a beautiful afternoon. It wasn't spring yet, really, but it was a little piece of spring. Everything was melting. Old peple could walk down the street without slipping and breaking their hips, and the very most hardest hearts melted

and got gooshy. All the melted ice made little rivers of
liquid, and floating down the little rivers were old pieces of
Kleenex and rotten scraps of cellophane that hadn't decom-
posed. All the trash was floating down the liquid rivers,
heading for the city sewer. There was a regatta of trash,
happily floating away, free of the ice traps of frozen, rained-
on mounds of snow under which they had been buried. Old
pieces of dog poops sat like damp statues, sitting there just
where they'd been plopped before the winter snow and ice
covered them up. It was a very poetic day.

Everything was melted, loose, and free. Everyone came
out of their houses and walked around. After all the ice and
snow in Boston during the winter, it was like a miracle to see
everything melting so fast. The sun was bouncing off everything so brightly that I wished I'd worn sunglasses. I was
glad when I got to the Hancock Street Bar & Grill, everything was nice and dark inside.

At the Hancock Street Bar & Grill, everything smelled
like stale beer and wet wool. I sat down at a dirty little table
that was all wobbly and ordered a beer. I felt kind of funny
sitting there all by myself at 3:00 waiting for Meredith. I
waited there at that little table until 4:00. This was not
turning out to be any great afternoon at all, I didn't think,
sitting there at a wobbly table waiting for Meredith.

Instead of beautiful music and cosmic love, there was only
a row of old geezers perched on bar stools watching basket-
ball on TV. I wished that I had stayed home at Jocelyn's
watching Jackpot Bowling. I decided to get out of there.

Just as I was leaving, of course, who comes in but Meredith
Greenberg. Was I mad. I don't usually get mad, but I was
mad. I stomped on outside like I didn't even see her. Actually I don't know why I was so mad. People can be late, and I
don't usually mind.

Outside the Hancock Street Bar and Grill, the dog poops
were all squashed, leaving brown streaks all over the wet
sidewalks. It was 4:00, almost time to get dark. I had wasted

my whole nice Saturday afternoon almost, just to come over here to the Hancock Street Bar and Grill, miles from Roxbury. I had missed some very good TV shows. I said to her:

"Am I mad! Let's get out of here!"

"Wait a minute, I can't go right now!" she said back to me.

"What do you mean, you can't go right now. I've already been here waiting for you for over an hour. What am I supposed to do now?"

"Oh, Cecyl, I'm sorry, but I just can't go right now. I can't explain; I don't have time. Just go ahead without me and I'll be over a little later. Come on."

"Meredith! If I knew this would happen, I wouldn't have come out! I'm going home right now."

"Oh, come on. You're a big girl. Just go over to this address (she handed me a little piece of paper with an address on it), and ask for Jean-Philippe. You'll have a great time, and I'll be there in about an hour."

I tried to make Meredith explain why she was treating me so rudely, but she would not listen any more. She was running down the street, getting into a car that was over-flowing with people. I could see her head sticking out the back window. She was yelling out the address and telling me to go to it. 685 Green Street.

Fuck you. Fuck you, Meredith, I thought. I don't usually think in such bad language, but this made me really madder than usual for some reason. I guess I was disappointed because I had looked it up in my astrology book and it said that it would be such a great day, and it wasn't. First, I had to take the MTA all the way over to Cambrige, and then I had to sit in a smelly old bar all alone for an hour, and then Meredith wouldn't even go with me to the stupid old party.

I stomped down to the MTA stop, and was all set to put my money in the thing and all, but for some reason I stopped. I stopped, and it was like the other side of my self took over. I looked down at the address I had on the crum-

pled piece of paper that Meredith gave me. Jean-Philippe.
Probably some jerk, and I would have to go all alone and
wouldn't even know one solitary soul.

I don't know why I did it, but I turned around and went to
the address that Meredith wrote down for me anyway. 685
Green Street. I don't even know why I did it, but I went right
up to the door and rang the buzzer.

A foreign-sounding voice answered the buzzer. The voice
mumbled something into the intercom and then it buzzed
me up. I went up. When I got to the third floor it was pretty
quiet, especially for a party. I turned around and tried to get
out of the place before anybody noticed, but it was too late.
The foreign-sounding voice was calling to me from the
third floor landing.

"Halloah! Halloah. Don't go away, Jean-Philipe will be
right back."

Well, somehow or other I went up the stairs. I wanted to
be polite, of course, and that's very important. Still, though,
some women would have been worried about their safety,
being alone with a strange man or who knows what, but I
guess I worried more about being impolite.

I went up to the third floor landing. It was terribly quiet,
considering there was supposed to be a party going on. I
wasn't afraid that this guy with the foreign-sounding voice
would hurt me, but I was afraid that the party would be
really boring, the kind where six people sit around in a circle
chatting and being nice.

It was just after 4:00 by then. Time for the Grand Trine
of Venus, Neptune, and Jupiter to take effect, but something seemed to have gone wrong. It was time for cosmic
love and spiritual beauty, not time to get trapped into going
to a boring, quiet party. I felt guilty for thinking these
things, and went up to the third floor with a more Christian
attitude.

The voice at the top of the stairs said, "You must be
Meredith's friend, Cecyl." "Yes," I said. I didn't know what

else to say. The guy said, "Come on it. Everybody will be here in a little while."

The guy had a weird kind of a South American accent of some kind. I asked him where his home was, and he said Puerto Rico. He had long, straight jet black hair and a nose like an Indian, with a nice hump in it. He was just sitting there in the living room, which was empty except for some suitcases and some musical instruments and a very fancy tape recorder. He was just sitting there on the dirty gold wall-to-wall carpet by himself listening to some music on the tape recorder.

I didn't know what to say to him. I asked him how was everything in Puerto Rico. He said fine. I was afraid of Puerto Ricans because they liked women in tight skimpy dresses with their bazoombas half uncovered. I knew that they liked to do cha-cha's, and other fancy dances where the man is supposed to bend the woman over his arm.

Actually, I never knew any Puerto Ricans, but I had to walk past them sometimes on my way to U. Mass. They always said, "pussy, pussy," and things like that only more gross. This guy didn't seem like that, though. He was just sitting there by himself being polite. "They'll be back soon," he said. "They just went out to get some wine."

He offered me a seat on the gold wall-to-wall carpet, and poured me a glass of wine. Then he turned the speakers of the tape recorder so that they were facing my direction so I could hear more perfectly. "There," he said, "how's that?"

I had to admit that "that" was great. *That* was about the most beautiful music I had ever heard. This lone guy was sitting all by himself listening to some music that was better than good. It was the most beautiful music I had ever heard.

He was not even listening to DoWop or R&B or psyche-delic music. It was not exactly jazz or classical music, either. It's hard to describe what *kind* of music it was. The foreign-voiced guy said why were people always having to put things in categories, and that you couldn't always put music into categories. Speaking of categories, I hate to admit it, but this music was, truly, more wonderful than DoWop, which I didn't think could be possible, actually.

I asked the guy where the music came from, but he just said "God." I said, no, he didn't know what I meant, and that I meant who was playing it or who wrote it or something like that. And he said, no, that *I* was the one who didn't understand what *he* meant, and that *he* meant that the music really did come from God, and no matter what *anybody* said that was the truth. I didn't know what to say, so I said, "Oh." Then we just listened. We didn't chat. I hate chatting, so it was nice we didn't have to chat.

For me, it was like hearing music for the first time. I was kind of like listening and hearing and relaxing for the first time ever. It was neat. I didn't feel any more like I was in a solid, concrete body. I didn't feel any more like I was in Massachusetts. I didn't feel like I was even in the United States. There just wasn't anything solid any more, it didn't seem like. It was as if I had turned into a puff of smoke and was beginning to float away.

In a way, I had a kind of heavenly feeling, like I was being called back home by an archangel, home to heaven. Maybe the ice had melted too fast that day. Maybe it was just the Grand Trine of Venus, Neptune, and Jupiter. The ice had melted very fast, leaving puddles of water to walk on, float over, on your way to heaven. Things like this can happen when an invisible vibration passes over you or through you. All kinds of things can happen that wouldn't happen otherwise, but, still, they don't have to happen. Sometimes things don't happen; but sometimes they do.

Anyway, this floating sensation that I started to get listening to this music with this person seemed like a more natural state of being than the one I used to have. It was almost like all of a sudden a whole new sense had come over me. Just as this new sense was coming over me, Jupiter, Venus, and Neptune were making a Grand Trine pattern in the heavens.

It was heavenly, just like my book said. It was just turning out a little bit differently from what I had expected.

I sat there with this guy from Puerto Rico listening to music for a couple of hours. It turned out that his name was Mario and he was not really from Puerto Rico, and that he had never ever lived there even, but he said that his parents had been living there for two years and he liked to say he was from Puerto Rico just to freak out the people in Boston who didn't like Puerto Ricans very much.

Finally Jean-Philippe, the guy who was supposedly organizing this so-called party, came in. He had Meredith Greenberg stuck on to his arm like a muff. I couldn't believe it. She was giggling and acting really stupid like she didn't have a brain in her head. She and Jean-Philippe were speaking in French and Meredith was all chic-looking because she was in Paris for so long, I guess.

There were at least fifty people right behind them. They were all carrying jugs of wine and bottles of tequila. One guy came up to me. He was speaking in a Spanish accent, and he said to me, "Hey! I'm half zonkered!" But he was not half zonkered. He was all zonkered, and he passed out on the floor in front of me without another word. I was glad he did because I surely didn't want to speak to him any more.

Everyone started singing and dancing wildly as soon as they came in. Up and down through the hallway. A dental hygienist person even came with a cannister of nitrous oxide and everyone breathed it and laughed even more. It was wild. It was much more wild than drowning in a sea of love, and even though I was afraid of Puerto Rican guys who liked women with tight skirts and jiggly bazooms, this was the most fun I'd ever seen people having in my life.

Some of the guys that I thought were Puerto Rican were not. They were from lots of places all over the world, just like Meredith Greenberg said. There were lots of German people, and five or six Brazilians, and a few people from Argentina, a bunch of Italians, and one French guy, Jean-

Philippe, who kept saying "jooost callll me Pheeeeeel." Just call me Phil.

Some of the Brazilians started pounding out samba rhythms on the walls with spoons, and a bunch of other people were in the kitchen beating on pots and pans. They said that pots and pans were more political than walls. They thought that was very funny, and laughed and laughed, but I didn't because I didn't know that sometimes people in South America beat on pots and pans during political demonstrations.

Mario came up to me and grabbed my hand, and showed me the basic samba step. It was fun and easy, and we joined the samba line going up and down the hallway. It was very noisy, but none of the neighbors complained because they were all there, too, making noise and whatnot.

After a while, the Brazilians started beating the spoons and pots and pans at double speed. Everyone giggled and laughed and screamed even more, and sambaed down the hallway extra fast. The line went around and around, back and forth. It only stopped for emergencies when somebody fell over laughing. I couldn't understand why the whole world wasn't always this way. Why was this day, this moment, so much more fun than all the other moments? Why weren't all moments fun? I wondered.

In the middle of one samba trip down the hall, Mario tripped on someone in front of him who was doubled over laughing from nitrous oxide. Mario seemed to be falling in slow motion, three seconds that seemed to last for an hour. Very slowly, as he fell, his hand seemed to clench mine tighter as his foot tripped over the person who fell down laughing on the floor.

Very slowly Mario glided to the floor, pulling me along with him, while all around us the hysterical laughers kept trying to dance. We glided together to a gentle crash landing, in a forest of ankles and dancing feet. There on the floor, in the hallway, right in front of everybody's samba path, time seemed to hang just suspended, not moving at all. And even though it was very noisy and everybody was dancing like crazy, everything seemed to go all quiet and still, and Mario pulled me over and kissed me.

While we were lying on the floor, I touched Mario's face. Every inch, every pore seemed to have a life of its own. First he kissed me, and then I kissed him; and then someone fell over on top of us. It was "Phil" (Pheeeel). He just laughed and laughed. "Pleased to meet you! You must be Cecyl!" he said. Then he fell over on top of us along with about half a dozen other people, including Meredith Greenberg, although nobody else started kissing.

I didn't really care where I was then. It didn't matter. I was kind of like going away then, into a state of being of like going away. I was going away with Mario. Every second I was slipping further and further away. Away from Cambridge, away from Roxbury. There was no more Jocelyn, no more Mrs. Potter, no more Bipsy Street. I was drinking wine, sniffing nitrous oxide, and falling in love.

There was nothing to stop what was starting. It was like nothing else ever had been real. As if I had never been to Billy's Bar-B-Que even. The only thing that was wrong was that somebody danced right on my ankle when I was lying on the floor, and it seemed to be swelling up and turning colors. I had to go home.

When I got back to Jocelyn's it was time for the late news on TV. Jocelyn was sitting there in her bathrobe feeling cozy and watching the news on TV. I put on my bathrobe, too, and during the commercials I tried to explain to her what happened at the party, and how I had met my Soul Mate and everything; but Jocelyn just said, "Oh God" because she didn't believe in the Soul Mates theory.

I didn't actually know very much about the Soul Mates theory myself, but I did have a feeling that it was a true theory and that during my fall to the floor on the samba line I had met mine, my Soul Mate.

The next morning was Sunday morning. I watched religious programs on TV with MiMi, since that's all they had on. I sat there in front of the TV for the next five or six hours, just kind of staring at it, I guess. Finally, about 3:00 Mario called me up. I figured he would.

He didn't say much, just some words. But I was glad to hear his voice. He invited me to come over to his apartment again to listen to some more music. I did.

Over at Mario's it was just like it was when I first saw him the day before. He was sitting there all alone on the dirty wall-to-wall carpet listening to the tape recorder. The only difference was the weather. It was a rotten day, all cold and rainy and gloomy. But inside Mario's it was still the same. The music was so beautiful, and there didn't seem to be anything to say or do, so we just sat there together and listened. Nothing could be so beautiful as this music, except maybe for kissing Mario.

After a while Mario said, "This is starting to seem real to you, isn't it?" That weirded me out because how did Mario know that it didn't used to seem real to me but now it did? I always thought that the people in Cambridge were crazy for spending so much time trying to figure out what was real, and now here I was doing that same thing along with all the other weirdos.

Something that I liked a lot about being with Mario was that you didn't always have to talk in order for somebody to understand you. I didn't have to always be talking to Mario because lots of time he could just read my mind. That was a relief. And I didn't have to explain to him about invisible vibrations, either, because he could just *feel* them. He didn't have to look the vibrations up in an astrology book even. He could just tell what kind of a day it was going to be pretty often.

When I told him that I studied astrology and looked up the days sometimes, he just said, "that's a drag, Cecyl." He said that because he could just feel the vibrations, feel the day, and he said that you shouldn't need to look up a day in a book. I could feel the vibrations, too, but not always, and that's why I had to look up the days, still, sometimes. Sometimes I kind of had to strain to feel them, and it was easier to look them up.

When Mario felt like talking one day, he told me that he was the one who was playing the beautiful music on the tape recorder. He said that he came to Boston to go to music school with the rest of his band, but that they didn't like it in Boston or at the music school. They said it was a drag, and it was too hard for them to understand all the English.

There were lots of instruments hanging around the apartment. They were very beautiful and gleamy. Saxaphones, all sizes and shapes, flutes, a flugelhorn, trumpets, two pianos, lots of stuff. It never got stolen. Nobody ever tried to steal it. Mario could play almost all of the instruments there in that apartment, but he wasn't very good at flugelhorn or trumpet. Mostly what he loved to do was play the piano. He liked to sit at the piano all day and all night and write music. He would just hum to himself, and listen in his mind to what each different instrument was supposed to sound like. He was mostly always humming.

I liked Mario's humming. Pretty soon I felt bad when Mario wasn't around me somewhere humming. Pretty soon it got so that Mario *was* around me humming most all the time. Then it got so that it seemed like I couldn't even live any more without Mario being around me humming somewhere. Three weeks after I met Mario, I moved into that apartment on Green Street with him. I packed up everything I owned (which wasn't much) and moved right in.

To Live in Sin

MEANWHILE, back in the world, the War In Viet Nam continued and continued. And while I was busy falling in love and moving in with Mario, Dr. Martin Luther King, Jr. was being murdered in Memphis. Personally, I was very happy, but it was not going very well out in the world.

It wasn't going very well for Jocelyn, either. She was pissed off that I moved out, and she had a terrible time trying to find someone as nice as me to take care of MiMi every morning. Finally she gave up even looking for anybody and took MiMi right to work with her. She got over being mad at me finally, but it took a while.

The day that Dr. King was killed was one of the worst days in Jocelyn's neighborhood. It kind of wrecked the place because all the hidden anger and resentments that had been stored up for so long kind of like seemed to come loose, and the neighborhood started getting kind of scary.

About 4:00 we heard on the radio that Dr. Martin Luther
King was killed, and by 7:30 Roxbury (as the papers said)
"erupted in violence." There were lots of riots all over
Roxbury, and blocks and blocks were left in "charred ruins."

The only person who could get anyone to calm down was
James Brown, world famous soul singer. James Brown was
scheduled to do a concert at the Boston Gardens that night
at 8:00, but after the assassination and all the riots, nobody
knew if James Brown should still go on with his show.
He did.

It was a huge success. James Brown made everybody love
him and do what he said. He said calm down. I did not go to
the concert because I wanted to be with Mario, and Mario
said that rock and roll and soul music were very bad for
people, and that it was not music and that it hurt your ears if
you had any hearing sensitivity at all.

Anyway, I stayed home with Mario, and we watched the
Viet Nam War on TV. It was terrible, as usual, and I wished
that I could have seen James Brown singing "Hot pants:
make ya sure of yourself, hot pants."

All the rioters stopped and calmed down in order to go to
the concert, but the next day the riots started up again. This
time they got closer to Jocelyn's apartment, and she started
getting scared and went to stay with a friend who lived in
North Cambridge so that she and MiMi could be safe.

A few days later a White lesbian who lived near Jocelyn
was set on fire. Somebody threw gasoline on her and lit a
match. She ran to a store and begged the people to help her.
They did, but it was too late. She was too burned. She died
forgiving her torturers, and asked everyone else to do the
same thing.

After a few days, things quieted down again. Jocelyn
came back and waited to see what would happen. What
happened was that an after hours night club opened up
across the street. It was not a very good thing because people

got in fights. One night an elderly gentleman who lived upstairs in that building where the after hours club was got shot by accident when a fight broke out.

The fight started in the front hallway of that building. Then it moved up the stairs, and crashed right through the elderly gentleman's living room door, and finally spilled out onto the gentleman's living room carpet, along with small particles of the gentleman's left lung. He survived.

Despite everything, though, Jocelyn stayed there in that apartment for one more year before she moved to the suburbs; and she only got mugged once, and even then she only got hurt a little bit. But she also has gotten mugged once since she's moved to the suburbs, and that was on her way to work, walking from the MTA train to her office. There is not any way to be truly safe all the time.

During Jocelyn's last months in that apartment, the neighborhood got taken over by the Urban Renewal and Renovation Committee of the City of Boston. After Urban Renewal, all that was left was Jocelyn's apartment building, and an ice cream store that was over near the freeway. Aside from that, it was just razed ground for blocks, and even for miles, like Sherman's march to the sea. What Urban Renewal did was much, much worse than what the rioters did, for sure. It was very, very bad.

The Urban Renewal people said that they needed to tear everything down to make room for a new highway, but they never built the "new highway" at all. Even to this day that highway has not been built. All they did was to tear down a lot of people's apartment buildings and houses. All that was left was a bunch of empty lots and rubble.

I was so happy to be over at Mario's house. Not just to escape from everything in Roxbury, but because it was like living in heaven for me there, being with Mario all the time. I guess Mario kind of cast a spell on me or something, but I got to where I didn't, truly, want to live anymore if I couldn't hear Mario humming all the time.

Still, it did weird me out that I was in love and living with a black-haired musician from somewhere in South America, and lived in an empty apartment. Still, I was in love, finally, and it was very wonderful.

Sometimes Meredith Greenberg would come over with Phil (Pheeeeel). Phil lived there in that apartment on Green Street, too, but he was hardly ever home. I asked Meredith if it was weird the effect that Mario and his humming and his music were having on me. She said, no, that I was just in love, and that's what happened when you were in love, and that she knew that I would like Mario because we were so alike, and that's why she wanted me to come to the party.

I asked Meredith if it was bad manners the way Mario always was trying to kiss me all the time no matter where we were or who was hanging around to see him kissing me or me kissing him. Meredith said no, it wasn't bad manners, and that she saw people doing it all the time (kissing, that is, not "having sex") in Paris and it seemed just fine to her. Mario said the same thing. He said that they kissed all the time in Paris, and they kissed all the time in Rio, and he was going to kiss me all the time in Cambridge, too, unless I didn't like it or something.

It seemed that we "had sex" more than a usual amount, too, and in fact, I had a very hard time trying to get to my 8:00 a.m. class after I moved in because of always "having sex" when I should have been at the MTA stop already. That was bad, I guess; but it didn't seem like it at the time.

I guess we were pretty much either listening to music, "having sex," or kissing a good portion of every day. It got to be "normal" for us. It got to be part of a regular day. But, you know, it was strange to have an "us" in my life. The only other time I had an "us" was with Mom and Billy, I think. With the other people I knew, it was just "me" and "them." With Mario, though, I had an "us," and it got to be part of a regular day for me.

Mario's days were all pretty much the same. I guess mine were, too, but not as regular as his days. Mario hardly ever changed his schedule. First thing every morning (after we "had sex") he'd get up and go to the kitchen. He'd boil some water and make a little tiny cup of coffee with two big spoonsful of sugar. It was awful. Then he'd go to one of the rented pianos. (There was one in his bed-room and one in the kitchen.) On a normal day, he'd sit there at the piano and play or write music until it got dark, and then he'd stop and have something to eat and watch TV. That's usually all he ever did, except for smoke cigarettes and drink liquor, which he could do at the same time, of course.

Even though Mario came from kind of a world traveler family, he hardly ever went very far away from that apartment on Green Street unless he had to. He just kind of walked around in circles in the apartment: from the bed to the piano, from the piano to the refrigerator, from the refrigerator to the TV. Over and over.

Mario was the most quiet and shy person you could ever imagine. It was hard to understand how he could get out and perform in front of other people and be a band leader and everything, but he did.

Most of the guys in Mario's band lived in that apartment with him, too, but most of the time they weren't there. Usually, in fact, they only came "home" to practice their instruments. They did practice a lot, though. Lots of times all five of them would practice at the same time, too.

They'd go in their rooms and shut their doors, but you could still hear everything, only just a little muffled. I liked it when everyone practiced at the same time, for some reason, though. I think the neighbors liked it, too. They were mostly Hippies. The Hippies would even stop Mario and the other guys on the street and say things like "Hey, man. I heard you practicing last night. It was far out," and that would be nice.

Considering that Mario hardly ever left the house, Mario seemed to know a lot of people. That's because lots of people would come over to see him, and so he didn't have to go out to see anybody else. They came to him. Even me. I probably would never even have met Mario if it hadn't been for Jean-Philippe's party.

But it wasn't too lonesome for Mario because there were a lot of musicians coming in and out, practicing instruments and talking about "gigs." Lots of the musicians came from other countries and spoke foreign languages, too, and so they liked to talk to Mario because he spoke about four or five languages very well.

Mario had a very good education. When I compared myself to him, I could see that I didn't have a good education at all, but Mario said it didn't matter. In a way, it did matter, though, because I couldn't communicate with a lot of people who came over. I didn't know any foreign languages and I didn't know anything about "serious" music, either. I was a musical illiterate.

I guess it was OK like that for a while. Mario just spoke to me in English, and when people came over who didn't speak English, I'd just go read a book and sometimes bring them a cup of coffee to make them know I still liked them. After a while, though, Mario said that it "was getting to be a drag." He said that he would like to speak to me in Portuguese once in a while, and that it would be very easy for me to learn it since I already knew some French.

Well, I did take French at my high school in Phoebus, but I wouldn't say that I really "knew" very much French at all; and, besides, Portuguese didn't sound very much like French to me in the first place. But I tried learning some Portuguese anyway. Maybe it wouldn't have been so hard if the Brazilians who came over hadn't laughed so much when I tried to speak Portuguese. O well.

Mario knew lots of languages: English, Spanish, Portuguese, French, Italian, and some German. And a little bit of Dutch. He knew these kinds of things because he lived all over the world because his parents—his father, actually—worked for a Big International Company that had branch offices all over the world. His parents knew all kinds of rich people, and they were even a little bit rich themselves, I think.

Nobody told me that Mario's parents were a little bit rich,

but I guessed that they were. I don't know why. Still, even though I figured that Mario's parents were kind of rich, I also figured that it wouldn't do *me* any good, just like it didn't do me any good to have Meredith Greenberg pay the rent for a little while. Well, it did do a little bit of good, but it also did a little bit of bad, also, because I got spoiled. Anyway, I learned my lesson from Meredith Greenberg that as far as I was concerned, it didn't matter if anybody else could do me any good; I'd just have to do me my own good.

Another somewhat rich person who came over to see Mario sometimes was Wes Edmunds. Wes Edmunds was a pretty rich lawyer who used to go to "Harvard Law." Wes Edmunds spent half of his life in Rio de Janeiro, and the other half of his life in Cambridge. He thought it was fun to take care of poor artists' immigration problems, and so lots of Mario's musician friends from all over the world knew him.

One day Wes Edmunds dropped in. He said why didn't Mario and I come over to his house and see his home-movies of Rio that just came back from being developed. Mario said OK.

I asked Mario how come he said OK to Wes Edmunds when he hardly ever said OK to anybody else. He said it was because Wes Edmunds had helped so many people out with their papers that he wanted to be nice and do something to make Wes feel good; but Mario also warned me that it would be a very terrible "scene," and if I didn't want to come I didn't have to.

Mario said that Wes Edmunds was a real "biku," the type that they had a lot of in Rio. Mario said that that was why Wes Edmunds liked to spend so much time in Rio, because it was so full of "biku's." Biku is a word they used in Brazil for somebody who is very phony and superficial, but even though Wes Edmunds was a biku, said Mario, he was still helpful to "a lot of the cats."

We both went along to Wes Edmunds' house. I wished I

hadn't. It was just like Mario said it would be: very phony and biku. For two and a half hours Wes Edmunds showed "film footage" of one perfectly tanned, perfectly shaped girl in a postage-stamp-sized bikini after the next. They were all lying around on beaches or parading back and forth in front of Wes's camera. It was not "film footage" of Rio; it was film footage of belly-buttons and things. It was just like I was afraid the Brazilian men would be like, except that Wes Edmunds was American, and that just proves that anyone can be awful no matter where they come from.

I did not make a good impression. I felt like a stout old Russian peasant woman, accidentally stranded on a beach in Monte Carlo with a gunny sack for a bathing suit and a sack of corn cakes she was saving for the next day's dinner. It was not a good feeling. I wanted to go back to the farm in Russia where everyone was cold and miserable and there were no beautiful girls lounging around in bikinis. I sulked a lot until it was time to leave.

Even though I sulked, Mario did not get mad at me or act embarrassed. Instead, he just apologized for letting me come to Wes Edmunds' house. He just said that "most Brazilian biku's were like that." He said you just have to ignore them because they will never change in a million years. "Don't worry about a biku," said Mario, "a biku's nothing but a guy with a bunch of credit cards that don't care about anybody else unless they can do something for them." Mario said he would make it up to me, I would see.

Mario made it up to me by taking me to hear Vladimir Horowitz playing Chopin at Symphony Hall. I think that Mario spent his last money to buy our tickets. They were very expensive.

Mario said that Chopin's music was "from God," and that there wasn't anybody in the world who could really play it perfectly, but Vladimir Horowitz was as close to perfect as anyone in the world could be at the moment.

The night of the concert we got to Symphony Hall very

early. We had very good seats, as close to the front as we could get. It was mostly only "Old Ladies" down near the front in the expensive seats with us. They all had white or grey or blue or pinkish hair. When Vladimir Horowitz started playing, everyone began to cry because it was so beautiful. The Old Ladies all cried, and Mario cried very much, and I cried, too. But I only cried because everyone else was crying. It was very beautiful, and Mario would shake me every time Vladimir Horowitz was getting ready to play the best parts.

Every once in a while if Mario had a friend who was playing at a club somewhere, we could go out and listen to some music for free. Paying to go hear Vladimir Horowitz was something that we could not really afford. When we went out and listened to free music, though, I would be surprised by the way so many people would swarm around Mario and be so happy to see him. "Mario, what's happening, man," they'd say, and things like that. It was so many of them that it started to make me feel weird, and I had to start wondering if there was something more going on than I realized with Mario.

One day Phil (Pheeeeel) sat me down and had a "talk" with me. He said that I didn't understand that I was living with a musical genius, and one of the "greatest jazz musicians anywhere in the Western Hemisphere." I didn't know what to say to Phil. I did not know if what he said to me was true or not, even. But I was starting to see, for sure, that a lot of people did have that opinion of Mario.

I couldn't even have any opinion about Mario's music at all, since the only kind of music I knew anything about was Do Wop. I was just in love with somebody who wrote and played really beautiful music, that's all I knew for sure. So Phil sat me down another time, and tried to have another "talk" with me. He said that I should begin to realize that I was living with a great genius and that I should "encourage him to get out more." Phil said that all his talent would go to waste otherwise, because he was so introverted and all.

I still didn't know what to say to Phil. I started to feel very bad, though. All I wanted to do was be in love. All I wanted to do was live in that little apartment and go to my college. That was all. These things that Phil said made everything complicated, it seemed. All of a sudden everything seemed complicated.

At Mario's house I was warm and cozy. I was loved and petted, and kissed, and tickled, and smiled at, and talked to, and hummed to. In fact, I was having such a good time that I got a "D" in my 8:00 class. It was my very first "D" of my whole life in school. The teacher said that I did a very poor job, and she was so disappointed in me because I seemed so bright and eager to study the books on our list. At first I was. We were reading *Middlemarch*, one of my favorites. I loved *Middlemarch*; it was cumbersome and long-winded.

I loved the way George Eliot wrote. Instead of, for example, saying "women can be pretty different from each other" or something, she said:

> The limits of variation are really much wider than anyone would imagine from the sameness of women's coiffure and the favorite love stories in prose and verse. Here and there a signet is reared uneasily among the ducklings in the brown pond and never finds the living stream and fellowship with its own oary-footed kind.

I liked the way that sounded, and I hoped I would find my own oary-footed kind one day, but I was, still, only one of the ducklings in the brown pond and not a signet anyway. It seemed like it should be easy for me to find my own kind because I was so ordinary, but, still, I was kind of lonesome, even with Mario sometimes.

I just kept on going to U. Mass. and reading my English books that were so long-winded and cumbersome. I also liked the flowery way the Irish wrote books, too. They used many great words, like "gloomy." Once I started reading

Irish books, I tried using more words, too, but later I'd just forget and go back to normal.

I wished that I could have lived in Ireland back in the old days when poets came around to your house and stayed with you, and you gave them something to eat and they read you poems. That would have been great. My Irish books teacher said that I should be proud of my Irish heritage, but the socialists at my school said that you shouldn't be proud of your national heritage, only your class heritage. They said I should be proud of my working class heritage and not my Irish heritage. Anyway, I wasn't really a proud type person; I just kind of existed. I thought of Bipsy Street. He wasn't proud, either, even though his band was starting to get to be a little bit famous now, and you could hear him and his band on the radio. They sounded good, and I figured they must be starting to make some money. I wondered if Mario would like to meet Bipsy. I asked him, and he just said, "Of course not. That kind of music hurts my ears. I hate it. How could I get along with somebody who played music like that, Cecyl? No, no." I felt sad, sort of. I don't even know why because I hardly even ever saw Bipsy anymore anyway.

One day Mario was out, and I was there in the apartment alone. I got out one of my old favorite Do Wop records that I had in a box. Just as I began to listen to one of my favorite tunes from Hughie Hughes and the Hugos, who comes in but Mario and some "serious musicians." The serious musicians looked at him. He looked at them.

At first it was very embarrassing because the serious musicians didn't know what to say or do. But finally Mario said, "That's OK, Cecyl, I like it." And he started dancing up and down the hall to it, just like when I first met him, and all the rest of us followed him and danced, too. It was fun.

Sometimes those days I would get sick of serious music and want to have some fun and dance. I wanted to listen to my Do Wop records, but I got nervous every time I'd put a record of mine on to play because I didn't know if anyone's ears would hurt or if anyone would think less of me for doing it.

Sometimes Mario's music was overpowering in its beauty, and sometimes something a little less beautiful would have been fine. I longed to see Bipsy Street and Dalia. I longed for the old neighborhood in Roxbury (even though it was torn down). I missed Jocelyn and MiMi. I began to wonder how I got myself into this whole situation at Mario's, and I wondered how I could get out, too.

One day Jocelyn came over to visit me. I asked her if I could come back to live with her in her apartment again even though everything was terrible back there now. She said, "Cecyl, you know I'd love to have you come back, but you know how impulsive you are. You might just change your mind again within a few weeks and it would be upsetting for me and MiMi to have you just move in and out again."

I guess it was her way of saying "No" because if she really did want me to come back she would not have given me a talking to about being impulsive. She said, "Cecyl, don't you know you have a life of your own?" That got me to thinking. It did not, actually, seem that I did have a life of my own. Mom and Billy had a life of their own. Jocelyn and MiMi had lives of their own. Mario had a life of his own. But it did not seem to me that I had a life of my own.

Even though I was in love and it was extremely special, and special things were happening every day now, I began to get depressed again. Somehow I felt caught between Mario and his brilliant music and my own empty self, between Mario's existence as a recluse genius wino and my own kind of semi-non-existence. Unlike everyone else around me, I was just a common, every day person. I was not very brave like Jocelyn. I was not very talented like Mario. I did not have a career at all or even a job. All I had was reading my books and going to U. Mass. on scholarship, which gave me just enough to live on in Mario's empty apartment.

Then, too, I started noticing little things about Mario, like how he drank every day no matter what, and he never smoked less than a pack of cigarettes to go with it. It seemed that he couldn't possibly be very healthy with all that alcohol and nicotine and instant coffee and sugar and everything that was in his system all the time. Plus, he almost never went outside to get any fresh air.

I really began to wonder if it were all a Big Mistake. All of a sudden, I wanted everything. I wanted nothing. I wanted to go away. I didn't want to go away. I wanted to be in love. I didn't want to be in love. I wanted to live with Mario. I didn't want to live with Mario. I wanted to be alone. I didn't want to be alone. That's how I felt.

I remembered back to what the astrologer, Mrs. McKenzie, said about how I was going to get married. That was supposed to be pretty soon, too. If I stayed with Mario any longer, it would have to be him; and I'd be Mrs. Musical Genius Recluse Wino. That didn't sound too good, Mrs. Wino. I needed to believe then that Mrs. McKenzie was wrong, and that Mario would not be the husband that she was warning me about.

I needed to decide that astrology was a bunch of baloney, and so I decided to become committed to the belief that astrology was a bunch of baloney by selling my whole astrology book collection.

I had so many astrology books then that when I got ready to take them to the occult book store, I had to borrow a little wagon from a kid in our building because I had too many books to take in even two or three trips. I'd read a lot of astrology books.

When I got to the occult book store, and told them that I wanted to sell all my books, the clerk said:

"But you may want them later, tomorrow, a later time."

"No, I don't think so. I won't," I said.

"But they cost you almost $300.00. If you sell them, the most we could give you is about $75.00."

"Oh, that would be fine," I said.

Then I heard the clerk talking to a friend of hers who was in the store:

"She doesn't want them."

"No, she doesn't want to know."

"There was probably something she didn't want to think about."

She was right. I was tired of thinking about Mario and getting married or not, and I wanted to think it was a lot of hooey. I took my $75 and got out of there in a new frame of consciousness.

I decided to start my life fresh, and have a better and a newer attitude toward everyone, including Mario. I decided to be a free person, and live one day at a time without worrying too much. I lived one day at a time for about two months then before I got depressed and withdrew into my little shell again.

"You're just like me," Mario said one day out of the blue. "Alone, you just always want to be alone, but you don't know it, you don't see yourself. But, Cecyl, if you want to be alone to look inside yourself, you can. It's not a bad thing to be just with your self because that's how you know what is inside and not just what is outside."

I didn't know what to think when Mario said that. There was something about Mario. I don't know what it was. I don't know. But anyway, I didn't think it sounded very good to be somebody who liked to stay away from people. But it was starting to look like that was true about me, that I was happiest when I was alone, or just with Mario, even though he was a wino. I guess I never did learn Portuguese just so I wouldn't have to talk to so many of the people who came over to visit. That way I could just wander off to the bedroom and read my books and nobody would mind too much.

In some ways Mario and I were like two peas in a pod. I

would hide away from the world and read my books, and he would hide away from the world and write his music and hum. We stayed there together for hours and hours reading and humming. I guess the main difference between me and Mario, except for his talent, of course, which I was starting to get sick of, but the main difference was that I never hummed. Sometimes Mario read books, but I never hummed. I was not very musical at all. Even Billy said that. He said, "Cecyl, honey, you can dance, that's for sure. But you cannot sing worth beans." It was the truth.

But one other difference between me and Mario was that while he hummed and wrote music and played the piano, he smoked cigarettes and drank wine or Scotch. When I did my reading, I never ate, or drank, or anything. I just sat there.

I guess I started to get sick of just sitting there reading in a bare apartment. I began to feel dissatisfied in some ways, including the material way. I began to wish I had some things. Not anything in particular, just some things, any at all: a chair, a bath mat, a couch, a salt shaker. Like everyone else my age in Cambridge, I was living a Yankee Tenement life style.

But I tell you, I was getting sick of it. I finally began to see what Meredith Greenberg was talking about. I did not have enough money, and I was an oppressed person from a poor area of the country. I did not know what to do about it except to go back and be a janitor again, and I didn't want to. I started to think that if Mario had more money, at least as much as me, it could be a little bit better than it was. At least we could get a bath mat or salt shaker. I didn't have very much, but I had enough to pay my rent and buy food and also a bath mat or a salt shaker. Mario hardly even had enough to pay his share of the rent, and he was always having to ask his parents to help him out.

Sometimes the only time Mario made any money at all during the week was on Sunday night. He'd go and play for $15 in this big restaurant at Harvard Square. All of Mario's friends would come down, but they'd come down after dinner and just order one beer or a cup of coffee. That wasn't very good for the restaurant's business.

To make things worse, when Mario would start playing, everyone in the place would get real still and quiet so that they could listen to Mario playing. But nobody ordered anything from the waitress. Even the waitress, in fact, stopped what she was doing and listened, too. No forks were clinking. Nobody was talking.

The owner never made as much money as he thought he would, considering the place was always packed and everything. So Mario would get a standing ovation from all his friends, and then he'd get his $15 and come home all depressed. It was awful.

I said to Mario one day why didn't he do some, just a little bit, of commercial music, just to make a little bit of money once in a while. "Cecyl," he said, "it would be like prostitution, like prostitution. You think that women with their sex are the only ones who can be prostitutes? Shit."

So Mario kept his music all pure. But part of the reason he kept it pure was because he always insisted that he have everything his way musically if he played with any other people. The trouble was that the only people who always let him get his own way musically every time were people who didn't play as well as he did, and he didn't like to play with people who didn't play as well as he did, so he only usually did lots of solos and then let the other people play their own solos.

But it did not seem like a very good trait for someone who was supposed to be a musician, to be someone who liked to be alone so much and not work in a group. I couldn't understand how Mario was ever going to make any money sitting in his room humming; but I figured something would turn up, since so many people thought that Mario was a great musical genius and everything.

I guess part of Mario's problem was that he was just so

protected growing up with parents who would just let him sit around and hum and write music all the time. If he had grown up filling salt and peppers and sweeping the floor, he might not have minded so much playing in some normal little place where there were just normal little people. That's what I was thinking at the time, but I guess it wasn't totally right what I thought. But some of it was.

One time I said wouldn't it be nice to do something to make more money so we could buy just one thing once in a while and have some more warm clothes for the winter and all. He said, "like what, be a janitor or something?" That hurt my feelings because I *was* a janitor before I met him, and being a janitor wasn't too low for me. Mario realized what he said and how I felt about it after it was too late. He stopped and thought for a minute, and then he said, "Ok, if it was good enough for you; it's good enough for me." Mario and this guy he knew went out together the next day and got under-the-table janitor jobs.

For a couple of days they thought it was funny, walking around in their janitor outfits and everything. They got jobs at a women's clothing store. But after a few days you could see that Mario was really ashamed of himself deep down for being a janitor. So one day he pretended he was sick, and he just never got around to going back to work again, even to pick up his check or return his uniform, so all that he did was to buy a janitor's uniform for himself and leave it in the closet. Large deal.

The next thing he tried was giving music lessons. That flopped. All that he did was sit and play for his students. He didn't teach them anything. It was just like little private concerts, and if the students stayed one minute over their time, he'd just get up in the middle of everything and make them go away. He was not a good teacher.

Then he and this guy named "Mike" tried making money by "transposing" music for this terrible band called "The Imaginations." The Imaginations were made up of a bunch of spoiled rich white boys who wanted to be stars and thought they could buy their way to the top. They were disgusting people, and bossed Mike and Mario around terribly when they were trying to adjust all the written music they had and adapt it to their different instruments. The Imaginations just thought everyone lived to be their slave. In the end Mike and Mario got cheated out of half the money that The Imaginations owed them. I said to Mario he should fight them to get the money, but Mario said it was a waste of time and he didn't have any time to waste on working for them or collecting his money. O well, I said to myself.

I still wanted to have some warmer clothes for winter and a bath mat or something. I got it in my mind even that I wanted to move into another apartment so that things could be nice and pretty and clean and regular. I wanted it to be more like it was at Jocelyn's when we had plates with flowers on them and hung our sheets out to dry and made them smell fresh. I said that to Mario, that there were some things that I was wishing for.

I was kind of surprised, but Mario said he would like those things, too. He said he would also like to live in a clean, pretty place. I said I wondered how we could pay for something like that ever; it would cost too much. But Mario said it was important, and we should go ahead and do it, and that we'd just have to try to get the money somehow or other. So we agreed to move into a clean pretty place with no ugly wall-to-wall carpet, and we agreed that we would get a bath mat because it had become a symbol in my mind.

We agreed to find a new place to live and start our lives all over again. All the places that Mario liked cost way too much money, though. I told him we could never afford any of those places in a million years, and was he crazy? But Mario said there was no point in moving in the first place if you weren't going to make an improvement somehow. He said, well, "we will just have to swallow our humble pie and ask my parents for some money." He did ask them for some money, and they sent it.

We moved into a lovely, decent brick apartment in a big apartment building. There were flowers and vines and trees and shrubs decorating the place, and there was a person to shovel the snow off the sidewalk in the winter. It was all lovely and quiet—except for Mario and his friends.

The neighbors began complaining almost as soon as we moved in. The management of the building said that Mario could practice and play his music and that it was OK, but only at certain times. I thought that this would make Mario mad, but it didn't. He said OK, he'd just play when the schedule said it was his turn. When he couldn't practice or play, he'd just hum and write down what he was humming sometimes. He hummed constantly after that. Hum hum hum hum. It was kind of weird but nice, still, as I always did like Mario's humming.

Well, that was how Mario's parents started supporting him, paying his rent and food. I paid for my half with my own scholarship money, plus I cleaned one person's house every week and baby-sat on Saturday afternoon. It was just enough to have a normal little apartment, and I didn't have to drop out of school. Still, we did not have enough money to buy any new plates with flowers on them, or even a bath mat. And all of our old pieces of junk looked even worse in the new apartment, but our new apartment was a little on the "biku" side anyway, though, I guess.

After Mario's parents started paying his share of the rent and stuff, though, it seemed like Mario even quit trying to make any money of his own. All he ever made was the $15 he always made on Sunday nights when he'd come back all depressed from playing. He said the only way he was ever going to make any "serious" money was if he moved to New York. I said what was the matter with that, and that there were lots of things to do in New York, and that it was very exciting there. He said that I didn't know what I was talking about, and that it was terrible in New York, and that I would hate it, too, if I knew what it was like.

He said that he could only make money in New York because that was the only place where the jazz business was big enough to make a living on, and that that's what he'd have to play if he were going to play: jazz. He said that he could "write charts" and play in studios, and that they had lots of studios, and that he could always be a "studio musician" if worse came to worst.

One day Mario had to decide for sure if he really could stand to move to New York, because his parents said that they were not going to keep on sending him money forever, and what the hell was he doing up here anyway and why didn't he come back down to Brazil anyway because it was so nice and warm and they missed him so much and didn't he miss them?

For a while Mario didn't know what to do. He couldn't get away with saying he was a music student anymore. Even when he was a student, he only got a bunch of F's. And then he didn't want to "prostitute" his music, and all there was for him in Boston was "prostitution music." He didn't know what to do or where to do it.

He thought of going to New York because of money. He thought of going to Copenhagen because the people there liked jazz, he said. And he thought of going to Rio de Janeiro because his parents were there and it was beautiful and warm and there were lots of good musicians there, he said.

That made me feel very weird. I just wanted to stay where I was right there in Cambridge and keep on going to U. Mass. till I finished. It took me long enough to get as far as I did, I didn't want to stop right then and there.

I just couldn't think of what I would do in Copenhagen or Rio de Janeiro. I thought it would be very beautiful, but I wanted to go to U. Mass. instead. You may think I was sick in the head for not wanting to go to Copenhagen or Rio de

Janeiro, but I didn't have enough money to go anywhere else but U. Mass. anyway, and it didn't seem like Mario could pay my way, either. Besides, I didn't see why I should change my whole life around and not finish my school just because of Mario, even if it was a good idea.

I guess it was dumb to miss an opportunity to go some place very exciting, but I just kind of promised myself that I would graduate from college, and I was afraid that if I went away I wouldn't be able to graduate from college. I was being narrow minded. I could have gone someplace else to go to college, too, and I could have learned even much more than I did at U. Mass., but, it would have taken a very long time to learn another language well enough to go to school and speak it. I might have ended up like Mario, dropping out because it would be too hard, and that would make it boring, too.

Plus, there was the money. How would we live? What would I do for work? Mario was no good at working; I already knew that. He was a great genius, sure, but what good did it do as far as paying rent went? None. Me, I was no genius, but I could get my own part of the rent paid, but Mario did not seem to think that was so important. I couldn't depend on Mario if we went away.

I needed to stay where I was, and continue doing my dumb old non-genius things. I wanted to read my books and write my dumb old non-genius term papers. That's all I wanted. Except I wanted Mario to stick around and quit drinking and act right.

Mario needed something more. He needed something else to do, and he needed some place else to do it in, I guess. I wondered what would happen. This didn't seem real. It didn't seem exactly ordinary enough for me. But Mario was going to have to decide soon because his parents kept saying how they were really and seriously getting sick of sending him money all the time. Making $15 a week at the restaurant just wasn't good enough.

Mario thought and thought of what to do. He said he liked the sound of going to Copenhagen. He said over and over that the people there really appreciate good music and liked jazz very much, and how wonderful it was when somebody appreciated you, and how people in the United States had no culture and how could they appreciate him: they didn't even understand what he was trying to do. But, then, he thought of how cold it is in Copenhagen and about how far away it is, and how he would have to stay with people that he didn't know very well until he got himself together, and how it all would take such a long time, and then he probably wouldn't stay there anyway, and everything, and then he started thinking of going to Rio.

He said that he missed his parents and that they were leaving San Juan, Puerto Rico, and going to Rio de Janeiro, Brazil where it was very warm and beautiful, although the music industry was very backwards, he said. He still didn't know what to do.

As for New York, Mario said that he would have his "best opportunities" there, but it was horrible to stay in New York all the time. And then he came up with the idea that he could go to work in New York and commute back to Cambridge when he didn't have anything to do. It was only 4½ hours by bus. That way, he said, he could make money, see me, and would not have to stay in New York all the time, and I could just stay where I was and finish school.

At first it sounded kind of stupid, commuting to New York, but when he explained it, it didn't seem as stupid. He'd only go to New York when he got enough work to make it worth while, he said, but "when I go it will be very important for the money." Mario said he wasn't sure he could take "being bossed around by New York biku's," but that he would be able to make lots of money in New York, and he would just have to face it.

Opportunity

YOU KNOW, it seemed like when Mario wanted to do something or have something, all he had to do was call somebody up. I didn't understand it, how he could just call someone up and ask them would they do something for him, and they would.

He called up this guy in New York named "Rico." He asked Rico if he knew about any studio work in New York. Rico said, "Oh, man, all you want, man. You know that, man."

One afternoon a man named "Benny" called Mario up. Benny was a very famous musician; everyone knew who Benny was. Benny said to Mario that Rico called him up and gave him the number because he wanted Mario to do some "studio work" for him. Benny said that he was "cutting" a new album in New York in about a week and could Mario be there.

Benny said that if it worked out there would be a lot of

money for everyone, and it was a good thing Mario was married to an American now so he could work legally and everything and keep "the tax scene together."

Mario said that he was not either married to an American and couldn't Benny be his sponsor so he could get his Green Card and not have to go through "the hassle" of getting married. Benny said that getting married to an American was a lot less of a hassle than going to the trouble of getting a sponsor. I guess that was Benny's way of saying "No." Benny said, besides, there wasn't time to arrange for him to be Mario's sponsor before next week, but he could get married and then he wouldn't get thrown out of the country at least.

Benny said, "well, what do you think, baby, there's no time to get it together with the sponsor thing before the gig." Mario said he'd "kick it around" and call him back.

Mario told me everything that Benny said and what did I think. I said that it didn't matter if we got married or not. I said let's just get married and don't even think about it too much. Mario said that something like that could be very serious for our relationship, especially since there was no such thing as divorce in Brazil, where he might be going to live if he didn't live in New York. I said that it would be more serious for our relationship if Mario never made any money. Mario said, "let's kick it around for a while."

After I kicked it around for a while, I said to Mario that the only trouble I could see about getting married was about the future, that nobody knew just what would happen to them in the future, and so how could you ever promise to do something for the rest of your life, no matter if it were legal or emotional or whatever have you. I told him that even for the sake of a Green Card how could I know if I could promise to *stay* married forever when I didn't even know what I was doing in five years? Anything could happen.

Mario said, "Of course, anything could happen." He said that no matter how you look at it, getting married was not real, that love was the only thing that was real. Mario said he didn't know if we should get married or not. I said maybe we could get married for a couple of years and see how it went. Mario said that this getting married thing was "bogus," but that I could always count on the fact that he would love me as long as he lived. He said that this was an actual fact and that I could believe it and trust it, but nothing else was real and nothing else could be trusted, but he surely did need his Green Card, too.

Two days later we got married at City Hall at Central Square in Cambridge. Mario called up his family in Rio. I called up Mom and Billy in Phoebus, and we all toasted long distance, and they sent up some nice presents. Mario said if we were going to get married, at least we shouldn't sneak around about it. We even had a little party, and we roasted a turkey and everything, and I got some loaves of bread from the North End, made by real Italians. It was good.

Still, it was an odd feeling. I remembered what Mildred McKenzie said about my horoscope and getting married and getting divorced. Here the first part of it was coming true, but, in a way, it wasn't a *real* marriage. I wondered if it were real or not. I wondered if it counted in my horoscope as a real marriage, or if I were still going to meet someone else soon.

The day after we got "married" Mario went to New York. I couldn't go because we didn't have the bus fare for both of us. I stayed home and pretended that I was on vacation to make up for it. I went to the movies every night, and slept late, as late as I could, and drank as much Lipton Tea with milk and honey as I wanted. It was fun.

Benny called up and said how come I didn't come along; you can't just get married and break up, ha ha ha. I said I was too busy to come, because I didn't want Benny to know how poor we were.

Three days later Mario came back early all of a sudden. He got fired. Rico called me up and told me everything that happened. It was because Mario wanted to have his own way on everything, and it was Benny's album and not Mario's album, and you couldn't always have your own way on someone else's studio time.

It didn't seem too bad, though, because Mario took home $900 for just two and a half days of work in the studio, even though almost all he did was get people mad at him. The sad thing was that it was his last trip to New York.

I guess we got married for nothing, since he never did go back to New York. He never made enough money to worry about "keeping his taxes straight." But when he came back from New York, Mario put a little sign over our front door buzzer: "Mr. & Mrs. Mario Rivera."

I thought it was very sweet, but I wondered what was going to happen because what kind of a marriage did we have if Mario wasn't going to go back to New York? It was supposed to be a fake marriage, wasn't it? When I asked Mario was our marriage deal real or pretend, he'd just say it didn't matter anyway. The only thing that mattered was love, and that I could be sure he would love me as long as he lived.

After that, I never knew what to say or what to think. I didn't see how anybody could really and truly promise anything for the rest of your life, including being married or even loving someone forever.

One day Wes Edmunds, the jet set lawyer who showed the home movies of naked belly-buttons, called up and said to me that it was very important that we had gotten married because now Mario could get His Green Card, and that I "would see the significance" of that in the "near future."

Wes Edmunds said why didn't we come over to his office and he'd get the "paper work rolling." Wes Edmunds said that things could "break" for Mario any minute and don't waste any time.

Things kept rolling along. One day soon that guy, Rico, called up. He was the one who knew Benny in New York. This time Rico said that Royal Carter wanted Mario to come audition with him. I tried to overhear as much of the conversation as possible because Royal Carter was easily the most famous jazz musician in the country, probably the world.

It was very shocking, but Rico said that he was out in Saugus, a suburb of Boston, and that he was getting ready for a week-long "gig" with Royal Carter at a club in Copley Square. Rico said that Royal Carter wanted to "check Mario out." It was an "opportunity of a life time." I thought that Mario would run out the door as fast as he could. He didn't. He told Rico that he couldn't make it, instead, because he didn't have a car and there was no way he could get out to Saugus.

About an hour later Rico was at our door. He was hopping mad. "Don't you think that some musicians would crawl on their hands and knees all the way to Saugus to audition for Royal Carter? Don't you think some musicians would crawl on their bellies?" said Rico. He was right, lots of musicians would have done that.

Not Mario. Mario just said, "Oh, man, come on. That cat is a drag. Everyone knows Royal Carter is an asshole. Biku." Then Mario just kept saying "Royal Carter is an asshole" over and over. Rico kept saying, "Holy shit, I don't believe you" over and over. Finally Mario went into the bathroom and pretended he was constipated in order to get away from Rico.

While Mario was in the bathroom, Rico said to me, "Cecyl, Cecyl, you've got to push him, push him. He's a great artist, but he don't wanna do nothin'." After a while it didn't seem like Mario would ever come out of the bathroom. We yelled and screamed at him. Finally he did come out, though.

When Mario finally came out he said to Rico, "Rico, man, you know I love you. You went out on a limb to get Royal to give me a shot and now I won't even go. I know how you feel about it." Mario explained to Rico that he was really grateful to have such a good friend, but that Royal Carter was just a "biku" in a way, and that Rico knew it, too, and what the hell was Rico doing all the way out in Saugus with a "biku" like Royal Carter, anyway.

In the end, Rico and I talked Mario into going to the audition "just in case." But Mario kept saying over and over that Royal Carter was a "jive asshole" and Rico should know better, but that he would go just to show me and Rico that we were wrong and that we were hung up on Royal Carter just because he was the most famous jazz musician in the world and what did that mean anyway. But he did go, and that made me and Rico feel better.

Mario and Rico didn't come back until it was really late. They were both very drunk. They said that they waited in the hotel lobby all afternoon waiting for Royal Carter to get out of bed and have the audition, but he never did get out of bed all day long even though he knew that Rico and Mario were waiting for him. He was having sex with someone.

Rico and Mario said that they waited for hours and hours before they gave up, and then they just stopped by some place for a "few beers." Rico passed out on our little couch right away. Mario and I went to our bed, and Mario passed out right away, too, but he never did say to me "see, I was right," or anything like that. But I'm sure he wished that he had been wrong about Royal Carter, but he wasn't.

The next morning it was Sunday morning. We were very low on food and money, but Mario and Rico and I put our coins together (nobody had any dollars), and we had enough to buy bread, eggs, and sausage (because it was before the Recession). We had a good breakfast and nobody talked about Royal Carter anymore.

That evening it was time for the free dinner at the restaurant where Mario would go to get his $15.00 and come home all depressed after his standing ovation. It was just another Sunday, but while Mario was getting $15.00 for his standing ovation, Royal Carter was getting who knows what for playing at the club at Copley Square. I think that made Mario more depressed than usual even though he said that it didn't.

Living With Adversity

PRETTY SOON my scholarship money ran out. We used it up too fast and it wasn't even the end of the semester yet. Mario's parents kept sending him enough money to pay for his share of the rent. My share was supposed to be paid for with my scholarship money, but we spent my scholarship money buying Mario a piano because he needed one so very badly. We figured we could afford it because Mario would be going to New York and then we would have enough to pay for everything. We didn't.

I told Mario it was alright; he couldn't help it if it didn't work out in New York and I would go and be a janitor again. Mario said, no, that no wife of his was going to be a janitor. He said he would try harder to make money. I didn't say anything, just to be polite, but I wasn't exactly a normal wife, was I? He wasn't exactly a normal husband, was he? We just happened to be married for certain reasons, weren't we? I wondered about all of that, but I was glad to hear Mario say that he would try to make some money.

At least there was one good thing about getting married: Mario didn't have to leave the country, so I could stay where I was and keep on going to school and not have to say good-bye. But the bad thing was that Mario never went back to New York again, and he never did make hardly any money.

I myself didn't know what to do about getting anymore money without being a janitor again. One day we completely ran out of money except for the penny collection that we scraped from the bottom of our pockets and inside the old couch cushions. We had just enough money for a stick of margarine and some Wonder Bread. It was just like George Orwell talked about in *Down And Out In London and Paris*. That was a good story, but I didn't like being in it.

We wondered, that day, if we would have anything else to eat for dinner besides margarine and Wonder Bread. It was Saturday late in the afternoon. It was almost like a miracle when Rico came in at 5:30 p.m. with a skinny little frozen chicken. He was holding it up by its little plastic bag that it was in. It was all bluish-pinkish-white and pitiful looking. "Hey, Cecyl, hola! Look what I got! Do you think it could be ready in about 30 minutes? I gotta meet Royal at the club."

Rico was so proud of his chicken. But I had to tell him that it was frozen solid and that you could never cook it in 30 minutes. Rico said that Royal still had not paid him, and that he was completely out of money, too, so we made some Wonder Bread toast with margarine and had that for dinner with some instant coffee and sugar, which we had not yet run out of.

Well, even though nothing much improved and we hardly ever had anything good to eat any more, I kept on going to college, and studying, and reading my English books. I still loved them so much, especially, still, *Middlemarch*, which everyone still always hated so much because it was long and cumbersome.

The normal thing for a married lady like I was supposed

to be, I guess, was to drop out of school and learn how to type and support my husband. My "husband," though, was a genius recluse wino, who developed his talent by sitting at home alone at his piano in artistic torture living on Wonder Bread and margarine. It was not a "normal scene," as Mario would say, but I hoped it would work out anyway. It didn't.

After a while I went back to being a janitor and kept on going to school still. I didn't even talk about it. I just did it, and Mario didn't have anything to say about it. He just pretended like it was not happening. He started playing some more gigs and he did make a little more money, too, but he spent most of that on liquor and it only made things worse.

I didn't mind helping to support Mario, but it didn't seem to make him feel good about himself, and so it didn't do any good. He started getting like I used to be with the television, watching it all the time. He had bought a TV with some of the money he made when he worked in New York and got his $900. He said that he needed a TV to relax with, and that he was always so tense and always needed the relaxation of television. He liked Westerns the best.

On his birthday, I bought him a set of TV headphones so I wouldn't have to listen to it any more, and then I could read my books in peace. Mario said that he didn't mind if I read books all the time; but he didn't know how I could stand it, and that it seemd "kind of like a drag" to him. He said, didn't I want to do something more creative?

It used to freak me out for some reason, and I never knew what to say or what to think about this, but Mario would say to me that I didn't realize that I had the same creative spirit that he did and that that's why we were together but I didn't realize that I had it, too, and that it was from God and everything.

One time he said it, and I said back to him that I didn't have enough money to do anything but read a book, and he said, OK, that does it, and he wrote a letter to his parents saying that some things had gone wrong, and would they please send enough money to keep us going for the next couple of months until he could straighten it out. They did.

When the money came, Mario paid all the bills and with the money left over he said he wanted me to take it and do something creative with it, whatever I wanted. I was weirded out, but I said, OK, I would take it, and I would buy some fucking ballet shoes and a leotard and tights and take some ballet lessons because only people like fucking Meredith Greenberg got to take ballet and I always wanted to take ballet. Then I felt better, it was always a sore spot, thinking about the girls at Radcliffe and their ballet lessons.

I was so excited, I was finally going to take ballet lessons for the first time in my life, just like the rich girls got to. The ballet class was taught by a crabby old Russian woman who was very little and muscular with long gray hair that she wound around in a bun on the back of her head down by her neck.

The Russian woman knew about Mario and his piano playing. I don't know how; I guess because of knowing some of the music students at the school where Mario used to go once in a while. But she asked me to ask Mario if he would like to play piano for her classes because she needed someone who had the "right feeling" to work with.

It was kind of nice, Mario played for our ballet class while we did our exercises, and he also played for the little ballet performances that "madame" had with her "troupe." Her troupe was very little and it was more stuff just like Mario was into. They would be all pure and perfect and nobody wanted to give them any money but lots of people would hang around "madame" because she was still a great teacher and choreographer even though she hardly had any money.

"Madame" never gave up, though, even though she was oldish. She wasn't a ballerina any more, but she organized performances and taught lots of people, and slapped them on the legs if they didn't do the right thing. It was very exciting to try to do something just right, just like Mario was always trying to do.

Still after a while I got sick of ballet, and I can't exactly remember why I did. I guess I realized that I could never get very far with ballet because I started so late in life. You needed to start ballet when you were still very little so that your body grew in the right way, and your legs would go perfectly in the right direction. My legs were too short, anyway, and when I started getting more advanced I never could remember what order we were supposed to do what in, so that when I did a set of exercises across the floor with the other people, I would have to stop because I would just forget what I was supposed to be doing and it was very embarrassing and "madame" would start yelling at me and everything.

After I dropped out of ballet Mario lost interest in playing for "madame" and "madame" could see that he had and so she asked him to leave. Then we didn't have any money any more again, except for what I could make at my janitor job. I started to wonder about Mario. I started to wonder if he was an alcoholic. It was a shocking thought, but I started wondering about it.

I started to keep a notebook of how much liquor and wine Mario drank. I jotted down the amounts that I could find out about. It was a lot. It was much more than it seemed like, just hanging around him. One day I asked Mario if he thought he was "developing a drinking problem." I would have asked him if he thought he was turning into an alcoholic, but that might have seemed more rude. But I began to think that the only thing really holding him back from being a total alcoholic was that we were so poor and he couldn't afford to buy all the wine or alcohol he wanted.

For a while, I thought that sooner or later Mario would quit drinking and get back on a more normal course of life and get a little more healthy. He didn't.

Women in Prison

ONE DAY a friend of mine from U. Mass. called up. She said
that there was a special program where you could get college credit for working at a job. She said the jobs were all
political jobs and that it was all political and she could get me
into it because somebody dropped out right in the middle of
the semester, and there was nobody to take her place.

I thought about it. It would mean that I would have to
stop taking my English book classes and go to a job. But it
seemed like a good idea, because it seemed like I would have
to just hurry up and graduate and do something different in
life for a change one day. I guessed that making that "one
day" happen right then and there was OK.

They sent me to work at a place called "Libra." (I am not
making this up, just because I was into astrology or anything.) It was a place that helped women prisoners to find
places to live and jobs when they got out of jail.

When I got to Libra, I didn't know what to do to help

anyone find a job or a place to live. I had never even met any prisoners before. Everyone else at Libra knew what to do, but nobody seemed to know what I was supposed to do. It was like everyone forgot about me, but they did say that they believed in "loose structure" there, so maybe that's what it was.

At Libra I met a lot of nice people, nice women. The director of Libra was a woman named Lynn Ellen Bradshaw. Lynn Ellen knew everything to say to everyone there. She tried to teach me what to say and who to say it to, but she couldn't. All I could do, it seemed, was to hang around and visit with everyone and read reports. There were always a lot of reports there.

One day Lynn Ellen called a meeting. She said we were going to write a report on women in prison. She gave everyone a chapter to do some research on, but I was too afraid to do mine. I told Lynn Ellen that I couldn't do mine because I didn't have a car to collect my "data" with.

It was all right. Lynn Ellen knew that I was a chicken and didn't like to talk to too many strangers and that I was afraid to go into the prisons and everything. But, she was stuck with me on her "staff" and so she said, "well, we have to do something with you. Why don't you do some writing?"

I told Lynn Ellen that I could not do any writing, that my writing was very boring. But Lynn Ellen said that she bet I could write just fine and here why didn't I take these rough drafts that the other people all wrote and "make them sound like they were written by one person." Lynn Ellen said, just give it a try.

I gave it a try. It turned out alright. It turned out much better than I thought, and you couldn't even tell that it was written by more than one person. We all got to have our names on it, and we got it published by a big company, and we felt very proud.

I used to tell Mario about the women in prison and about everything that I heard about at Libra. But he would just say that if I were really serious about the poor women in prison I'd be a "Communist" because they were the only ones who had anything "real" to offer the poor people. He said what good did a report do, anyway. He said that people were usually in prison because they were poor and fucked up, and that's all there was to it.

That's just what our report said, too, but Mario refused to read it, although I don't know why not. Mario said that I didn't know what really and truly poor was. He said that I had never seen, never in my life, had seen anything as poor as he had seen in the other countries where he lived and that I should quit acting like a "silly hippie" if I were really serious about helping the poor people.

Mario said that there were millions of poor women who had to work as maids in other people's houses and had to live in other people's houses. And these women's children just had to go live with awful men in little hovels and sell Chiclets out on the street and beg.

I didn't know what to say to Mario then. I only went to work at Libra anyway because I was a poor person myself. I just wrote the report up like as if one person wrote it because I didn't know how to do anything else and because I was not good at talking to people in person and that Lynn Ellen was just being nice to me and letting me do that so that she would not have to fire me. But I did not know what to say to Mario, so I just said that I felt sorry for the poor people everywhere in the world, including myself.

I guess I was starting to get sick of Mario. He was making my life worse, and not better. Even though it was nice to be in love and have a boyfriend of your own, I was getting sick of him anyway. I would have done much better being all by myself. I could have stayed home and read my books and budgeted my money and made it last all semester. I could have had a nice simple life, but no, I had to be in love. That was the whole trouble, just like that book by Alice Walker said in the title, *In Love And In Trouble*. That's right. It was my own fault, though. And I had nobody else to blame. I wasn't pregnant, but I sure was in trouble.

One day I came home from Libra and Mario wasn't there. I could hardly believe it. He was usually always there. He came in soon, though, and announced that he was going away on tour with Eva Moreno, who was a very famous jazz singer from Brazil.

People all over the world knew about her, and she was always travelling all over the place, even to "Communist" countries where usually you're not allowed to go. She was a very good singer, although she did sing commercial songs, too. I asked Mario how could he go on tour with someone who was commercial? Mario said that it was true that she had lots of biku's in her audiences, but that he was going to be Eva Moreno's "music director" and that she had told him that he could write whatever he wanted to write for her. He said that the band was going to have "musical integrity," and then he passed out. He was very drunk.

I looked around me. Our apartment was a mess. There were cigarette butts everywhere and clouds of stale smoke hung around making it look like smog in some big city somewhere. There were empty pint bottles of Scotch everywhere along with torn up pieces of music paper. I wondered if it would always be this way, or if Mario would really go on tour with Eva Moreno. I sat down and cried and I wondered.

I called up Arletta, a friend of mine from Libra. Arletta had been a woman prisoner, but I never could think of anything to help her, but she did think of things to help me, so I called her up. I told her how I was feeling and what was going on. Arletta said, "Well, why don't you just get out of there?" I said, how could I get out of there. She said, "Easy, just pack up some suitcases and come over here."

The next morning, after Mario got over his hangover a little bit, I told Mario that if he didn't quit drinking I was going to move out. He didn't quit. It was pretty nice at Arletta's. I felt sad anyway, though. I tried to keep on going to my job at Libra, but I just felt like crying too much of the time, and I'd just come back home again so I could cry alone. Arletta was nice. She said, "just go out a little at a time. Work your way up to it."

One day Arletta came home looking all white, even though she was Black. Arletta said, "Guess what." I knew from experience what that meant. I said, "Oh, you're pregnant." She was. Arletta didn't have a baby, though. She had an abortion.

It was pretty sad, though, because Arletta was the romantic type, but this time I didn't say anything or give any advice about what she should do about it or anything. I just couldn't go through everything I went through with Betty Baines and all. I wasn't the one who got pregnant, either, so I just kept my mouth shut and said I would help her do whatever she wanted to do.

Arletta decided all on her own to have an abortion. I just sat and listened while she thought out loud. Then we went together to this clinic out in the suburbs. After Arletta had her abortion, she didn't feel so good, and she went to sleep for a couple of hours. Then she got up and we went home. In a few days she was almost all better and she didn't have any complications except for feeling kind of delicate.

After that Arletta and I decided to be stronger.

I went back to my job at Libra and made myself talk to the people a little more. I talked to one woman who had just gotten out of jail. She had shot her boyfriend, but she did not kill him. She said that he would get drunk and come over to her house and act nice at first but then he would get mean and then he'd beat her up and she got sick of it.

The woman told me that one day she just lost her mind, kind of, and went out and got a gun and shot him. She said it hardly hurt him at all, though, because the gun was too little, and barely even stopped him from hurting her at all much. She said that a white woman wouldn't even have been sent to jail at all, probably.

I told the woman that I had a boyfriend who got drunk all

the time too, and then this woman told me that I should go
to a thing called "Al-Anon." It was like an Alcoholics Anony-
mous for people who had alcoholics in their family. I found
that I could not help this woman find a job, but that she
could help me get to an Al-Anon meeting.

She was nice. She picked me up in a borrowed car and
drove me to the meeting. The people there were all very
nice, and they had a lot of phrases that seemed to make
everyone who went there feel better. They kept saying
things like "Let Go and Let God." They said that if somebody was an alcoholic, they had an illness that you were
powerless over. They said all you could do most of the time
was to "mind your own business." I tried to do that.

Since I had already moved out, I didn't have to go
through that again, but I did have to go back and get the rest
of my stuff, including my symbolic bath mat, which I paid
for with my own money and he didn't even care about
anyway. I found the bath mat in a dirty heap in the kitchen.

The place looked worse than ever when I went to get my
stuff and looked around to see what happened when I
wasn't there to clean up anymore. Mario didn't look too
healthy, and he said he was not going on the road with Eva
Moreno. "It didn't work out," he said. He said he was going
to go to Rio de Janeiro and spend some time with his
parents, who were living there then. Mario said it would be
OK because he had some friends there who were playing
gigs in nightclubs for the biku's from the jet set, but at least it
it would be something to do.

I missed Mario terribly, but Arletta and I got along fine.
She got a job working at a day-care center, and I kept on
working at my work-study type thing at Libra. Our *Report
On Women In Prison* turned out to be pretty successful. Lots
of people read it, and we even made some money on it.

After that, I got some work doing "rewriting" for people,
and I also learned how to write little newspaper articles and
things, so that I always had something to do. I liked reading

better than writing, but since nobody would pay me to read, writing little things like I was doing was good enough. I could sit alone and look at words, at least. I guess it wasn't the greatest thing in the world to do, but it was something. I sure did miss Mario, though, drunken bum though he was. I missed all his humming and his music terribly.

At Christmas time I missed him the most, but I did like being at Arletta's anyway. For a present, Arletta paid for me to go to a "psychic reader." She said it would help me take my mind off Mario, and that he was a drunken bum anyway and he lived half way around the world now, too. I said, Yeah, I know. Arletta even took me to some more Al-Anon meetings, and they tried to help me, but I was still getting depressed.

I remembered about what the astrologer, Mrs. McKenzie, had said about my getting married and then getting divorced and how it was all going to be because of me. It kind of weirded me out. I had pretty much forgotten about that, ever since I sold my astrology books and everything. Anyway, I was very excited to go to the "psychic reader."

Holiday in South America

THE "PSYCHIC READER'S" name was Mrs. Waters. Mrs. Waters was short and round and very dark black. Arletta said that everything Mrs. Waters said came true, and that lots of her friends had gone to see Mrs. Waters, and I'd see the truth of it.

I liked Mrs. Waters the moment I saw her. She just had this very nice and friendly and tired look. It was a kind of look of being tired from having done your best all your life. She was about 65 years old. She said, "Come on in, darlin. Sit down here by me."

She sat me down at her dining room table. She had a candle that she lit for me, and a Bible. She said a prayer to Jesus, and read a few lines of the Bible. Then she gave me a little bit of some nice smelling oil and told me, "Go on, rub it in your face and your hands. Go on. It won't hurt you none."

After I rubbed it all around she said, "Good, there, now we can start." She called on God to help me in my darkness. Mrs. Waters said that I was going to have to "take it easy" or I

was going to have a heart attack "at a young age." She told
me that I loved people too hard. "Don't love 'em so hard,"
she said. "You love 'em too hard."

Then she said, "I see you're gonna go see your mother for
Christmas, aren't ya. You got a message coming within three
days and it's gonna have some money in it fer ya so you can
go see your mother for Christmas. Money in a message so
you can see her."

Well, I was thinking of going to see Mom and Billy for
Christmas, and they said that they would send me some
money. But I hadn't decided for sure. Then Mrs. Waters
said, "I see it just like it's in front of my face. You walk in
through the front door and there's a little desk with a pile of
letters on it. And then you walk in through the dining room
and you see the windows at the end and you can see the
water there and a big hill, can't you? Must be a beach, a lake,
or something like that, huh? I can't see the bottom where
the shore is, though, only the blue of the water and the
green of the hill right by each other."

I thought about Mom and Billy's house in Phoebus. It was
near the Chesapeake Bay, but there was no way you could
see the water from Mom and Billy's house. And there wasn't
a hill around for miles. I didn't say anything to Mrs. Waters,
though, that would have hurt her feelings and make it
sound like her reading was wrong, though. I didn't say
anything bad about Mrs. Waters' reading to Arletta either,
since she paid for it and everything. I didn't want to hurt
anyone's feelings, but it did seem like Mrs. Waters' reading
was a waste of money except for the nice smelling oil she
gave me to rub on myself, and the nice praying she did for
me. That was very nice.

The next day Libra closed for the holidays. Arletta was
busy baking fruit cakes for her relatives who lived all over
Boston. Most of her relatives lived right nearby her in Dorchester, though. Dorchester was the next part of Boston
over past Roxbury. It was very big and spread out and not

very rich. Arletta said that this was like her relatives were: big, spread out, and not very rich. Arletta said her relatives were nice, though, and why didn't I stick around and have Christmas with them?

I didn't know how I felt about Christmas that year. I went to bed and had a funny dream. In this dream, nothing had much of a shape, but everything had a very wonderful color about it. It was a dream of all colors. All the wonderful colors came swarming over me, and then they swarmed away. It was a beautiful feeling.

When I woke up the next morning, I still didn't know what to do about Christmas.

Libra was closed, and I didn't have anything to do except read my English books, and I was good and sick of that. I didn't want to stay in Boston any longer. I was sick of Boston. And I really didn't want to go see Mom and Billy because they would feel sorry for me getting split up from Mario and everything. They were nice, and all, but I just didn't feel like visiting them right then.

That next day after my dream, I didn't do much of anything. I kind of just hung around. At about 5:30 a telegram came for me. It was from Mario. It said that there was a ticket waiting for me at the Pan Am office and that it was all paid for and would I please come to Rio for Christmas? I did.

It was a lot of trouble to hurry up and get a passport at the last minute and everything. Mom and Billy said please be careful because there were cruel military men down there who tortured people all the time and didn't even care how much it hurt them or anything. But I told them that I would not be getting in any trouble with any governments, and that I would be fine, don't worry.

I didn't get on the plane for Rio until the day before Christmas. I was feeling kind of bad because I never had learned any Portuguese at all. That's what they spoke in Brazil, Portuguese.

We stopped in Caracas, Venezuela to pick up some more people and refuel. The weather was much warmer than in Boston. I got out of the plane to look around at Caracas. It was just like this weird dream I had. It looked like the airport was on top of a big black volcano and everything was looking just like swirls of color with no shapes because we were right up in the middle of a bunch of low-hanging clouds. The clouds were all around us, and you could look down and see the beach. It was black, the sand on the beach was black; and the water was blue, bluer than any water I'd ever seen before.

When I saw Mario again it was just like before, just like I'd just seen him a few days ago or something and like nothing weird had happened or anything. Mario and his dad picked me up at the airport. I couldn't speak Portuguese, and his dad couldn't speak English, so Mario had to interpret anything anyone said just about. Mario was just the same old drunken bum that I always had loved so very much. I don't know why I loved him so much, but he was a special person.

Mario's father was a completely different kind of person. He was tall and thin and very distinguished looking. Mario was short and more of a dishevelled kind of person. It didn't seem that they had much in common, but you could tell that they loved each other a lot, and his father was always nice and polite and understanding with him. He never put Mario down for getting drunk all the time or because Mario was a bum.

After we picked up my suitcases at the airport we drove through the suburbs of Rio towards the inner part of the city where Mario's parents lived. The suburbs were full of terribly poor people. It was not like neat, American suburbs full of houses with boring green lawns. The houses in these were only cement cubicles built by the government. There were also lots of plain old shacks, much worse than shot-gun shacks that they had in Phoebus.

But the closer you got to the inside part of Rio, the nicer

and richer everything got until you got right up by the beaches and the water and the expensive jet setter apartments on Copacobana. The beaches were dazzling. There were all these white, sandy beaches right in front of the city, all over the place. There were little inlets and little white sandy beaches, and big alcoves and big sandy beaches, and palm trees and beautiful hills full of every kind of vegetation you could imagine. And the apartment buildings where the rich people lived were right on the most beautiful beaches and had palm-lined streets and pavement with designs in it.

Mario's parents lived right there on the beach in one of the very beautiful buildings. Their building was not so fancy. It was older, but in a way more beautiful than the jet setter apartment buildings at Copacobana. Mario's parents lived on a smaller beach.

When we got to their apartment building, we had to get into a little elevator that opened right out into Mario's parents' apartment. Somehow nobody but you could get into the elevator at one time, and somehow the elevator put you out into your own apartment. You had to have a special key to get in so that nobody else could come in and rob you.

Anyway, when we got into their private apartment hallway, there was a little desk. You could see it as soon as you got out of the elevator. It had all the letters I ever wrote to Mario since he moved away to Rio. There was a whole pile of them. Mario's mother had saved them all, hoping Mario and I would get back together and have a real marriage still.

Mario's mother was so happy to see me. She had even taken some trouble to learn some English for me. She cried and said, "Oh, my beautiful daughter, my daughter." I kind of felt terrible that in a way I wasn't her real daughter, but just kind of a real good friend. I wished that I had been her daughter, though because she was a wonderful person. But I still liked Mom, too, though.

When she quit crying and saying "Oh, my beautiful daughter" we moved from the hallway into the dining room, where there was a beautiful view of the bay and of Corco-vado—this huge statue of Christ standing on the top of a very green hill with his arms outstretched to the world below.

I was pretty weirded out by this. Not just because it was so beautiful, but because it was the exact scene that Mrs. Waters had seen on the inside of her mind. "I can see it just like it was in front of my face," Mrs. Waters said. The desk and the letters, the water and the hill. You couldn't see the beach because the apartment was partly facing the beach and partly facing the hill where Jesus was. It was especially weird because there I was in Rio de Janeiro and Mario was there and it was all so unusual. It was not everyday letters that I sent that were sitting on the desk in the hallway, and it was not an everyday beach or hill that you could see through the dining room when you got through the hallway. It meant something, but I did not know what it meant.

That night it was Christmas Eve. All of Mario's musician friends were there for dinner. And so were some of Mario's parents' friends, and so was Mario's grandmother. They had all come to celebrate Christmas Eve and to meet me.

Mario's grandmother was very sweet and short. Every time Mario's parents moved to a new place, they'd bring her along and get her a little apartment near them and get a maid to help her out. They all got along so well and were so sweet to each other.

I guess everyone had been waiting for me to get there. I got there as early as I could, but I guess it was kind of late for the usual dinner time in Brazil, which was in the middle of the day. There were lots of wonderful, strange things to eat that I could not recognize but were very delicious. I was in a foreign country and it was Christmas Eve, and I was with Mario, and his parents, and his friends, and his parents' friends, and everything. It was so beautiful and exciting. I just smiled and smiled and hugged Mario a lot and he hugged me and it was all very wonderful.

After a while, I went into the kitchen for a glass of water. I saw this young woman sitting at the kitchen table all alone and sad-looking. It was awful to see someone sitting all alone looking so sad on Christmas Eve when so many other people at the dinner were looking so happy, including myself. I went back and asked Mario who was it who was sitting in the kitchen at the table all alone, looking so sad? He sighed, "Dona Irmelda's empregada ... my grandmother's maid. The maids are all called empregadas here." Then he said, "I know what you're thinking, Cecyl. There's nothing you can do about it, believe me. We all hate this shit here with the empregadas, but at least it gives them some place better to sleep than a cardboard shack that some people have to live in around here."

I was totally shocked. It was just like what Mrs. Matt from 6th grade said about the "Ten Good Things About Slavery In The Old South." It Christianized the heathen African and it gave them a place to stay.

I got very depressed all of a sudden. There was a sweet old woman at the dining room table who had a slave sitting back in the kitchen just waiting around till Dona Irmelda felt like leaving. I knew that the empregada had been sitting there for a long time, waiting for me to arrive so everyone could eat and she could get out of there. I didn't know what to say or do.

"We've all tried doing things to change the way it is for the empregadas here, me and the other cats," Mario said. "But not very many of the other people who pay the empregadas are too interested. But it's everywhere. It's everywhere. Most of the empregadas themselves, Cecyl, don't even want to change because they don't know what else to do." Mario said that you can't just tell the empregadas to go home because they don't always have a home to go to. "And you can't just invite them in to sit down for dinner because they don't want to," he said, "because they aren't really part of the family and they don't want to listen to all the bullshit that everybody talks, you know? It's a terrible thing, and," he went on, "see, Cecyl, that's why so many people in poor countries are Communists now, because there's no other choice that they can see." So that's why you had Communists. It seemed like there should be some other choice. Was that all there was? I wondered.

I went into the dining room and tried to keep smiling and letting Mario interpret things for me. It was very hard, because I kept thinking of the woman in the kitchen. I just wanted to sit down and cry because I never in my life wanted anybody to sit around and be miserable in their lives because of *me*. If only I could have gotten there earlier, she could be off of work by now. Damn me.

It turned out that Mario's parents had not one but two empregadas of their own, but they weren't there for Christmas because they had other places to go. One of their empregadas did the cooking and one did the cleaning. They both went out shopping and they both had rooms there in Mario's parents' apartment, but they didn't have to always stay in them if they didn't want to. You could say that they "lived out." But they could have "lived in" if they wanted to.

One of the empregadas had a baby. It turned out that Mario's parents were very nice to their empregadas, especially the one with the baby. They paid for all the baby's expenses and doctor bills and everything, just as if it were theirs. But somehow it still just didn't seem right, having servants and all. I didn't know what to think.

The next morning was Christmas morning. Mario and I woke up in the same bed. It was just like always. We kissed and hugged and had sex even though Mario woke up with kind of a hangover. But there we were in Rio. It was about 90 degrees in the shade in Rio on Christmas day. It was so exciting to look out the window and see the beach and the flowers and the streets lined with palm trees when I was just getting used to all the winter ice and snow in Boston.

And I was very excited to see Mario again, drunken bum

that he was. I asked if he wanted to go to the beach since it was so hot and beautiful out and everything. He didn't. I asked his mother and father if they wanted to go across the street to the beach with me. They looked at me like I was crazy. They didn't want to go, and they said it was too hot to go to the beach.

Still, the beach was right across the street, and after being in Boston where everything was all freezing cold and everything, who wouldn't have wanted to go to the beach? But nobody did. I decided to go by myself. When I walked across the living room in my shorts and a towel around my shoulders, heading out the door, Mario's parents came and stared at me like I was out of my mind. They looked terrified.

"Where are you going?" asked Mario's mother in terror.

"Oh, just to the beach for a little while," I said.

"You know, sometimes that is not a good idea," she said back to me.

Then Mario came out and tried to talk to me:

"Cecyl, you don't know what you're doing here. I'm telling you, there's lots of creepy guys, you don't know."

"Mario, what do you think is going to happen to me, a boogey man's gonna get me or something? I can take care of myself well enough."

I couldn't. I came back about fifteen minutes later. A whole bunch of creepy guys came over and sat in a circle around me on the sand, and talked about me in Portuguese, and one of them touched my hand. It gave me the creeps.

I couldn't take it and had to come back and eat my humble pie. Mario and his mother were waiting for me back at their apartment. Mario's mother was worried about me, but Mario just laughed and said, "I told you there were a lot of creepy guys around here, Cecyl."

I never went out alone again as long as I was in Rio. If Mario or his mother didn't go with me, I didn't go. I asked the empregada to go for me, just like everyone else, if I needed anything. I figured that the empregadas, at least, could speak Portuguese and knew where they were going. I didn't even understand what the creepy guys were saying to me when I went to the beach alone that day. I hope it isn't still like that in Brazil today. Sometimes men bother you when you walk down the street in public alone here, too, but at least I can speak English and I know where I'm going sometimes.

After I'd been in Rio for a few days one of the empregadas told Mario to ask me if I had any dirty clothes she could wash for me because she was going to do some wash. I wasn't used to being in a tropical climate, and my clothes were all dirty and sweaty. I gave her a whole big pile, including the sheets. She took all the stuff . . . and washed it out by hand.

I felt terrible because I figured she'd just throw them in the washing machine, but she told Mario that the washing machine could only be used some of the time because of the electricity coming into the building. I didn't understand, but Mario said you couldn't count on everything mechanical like you could in "the States."

The empregada didn't seem to care, though. It seemed normal to her. After the clothes were washed, she put them out to dry on the balcony under some rocks.

I couldn't believe it, rich as Mario's parents were and everything. I asked Mario why didn't the maid just put everything in a dryer after the electricity came on full blast again. He said he didn't think there was a dryer, and I didn't know if he knew what he was talking about or not.

I went out and got myself a Portuguese dictionary so that I could say some words to the maid. I asked her why did she dry the clothes out under a rock. She said, of course, so they wouldn't blow away in the wind. Then I asked her why didn't she put the clothes in the dryer when the electricity was working, and she said because you didn't need a dryer because the sun was so hot that everything dried very fast without electricity. Then she laughed and thought I was a stupe.

If I knew that the maid was going to wash out my stuff by hand and dry it under a rock on the balcony I would have done it myself and not have made her work for me, but it was too late by the time I found out what she was doing, so I just gave her some dusting powder I happened to have, and she seemed so happy, and not mad at all because she washed my clothes. In fact, the empregada seemed happier as a person than I was. She didn't worry about stuff. She just seemed to do her job and go away and have a good time. I didn't get it, but it seemed like all of the poor people of Brazil were like that. They didn't have anything, but they seemed like they had a better time in life than the Americans who expected so much more. It seemed to me that the more you had, the more you wanted.

So I asked Mario why was it that the poor people in Rio seemed so happy even though they were poor, but he just got really mad. This terrible look came over his face, and he said, "You think these people like being poor? Just because they can laugh and sing, do you think that they enjoy their suffering?

I tried to tell Mario that I didn't mean that. I told him that I didn't mean that I thought they were happy *because* they were poor, but that they were happy *even though* they were poor. But in a way, I guess Mario was partly right. I kind of was wondering if they were happy because they were poor.

Mario said that the poor people in Brazil were just trying to make the best of it because they didn't think that they had any choice, except for the Communists. He said that only the Communists were different because they did not accept poverty, and tried to organize the people to make things better.

I guess that Meredith Greenberg was trying to explain that to me, too, when she tried to get me to see that I was a poor person from a poor place, and that I should not accept it. But it was different being poor in America. In Brazil even the people who weren't so poor didn't have it as easy as many people have it in America. Mario told me that before, but it was hard for me to believe before I went to Rio.

In Brazil lots of things were very different, but you'd never have known it from those home movies that we saw that night at Wes Edmunds'.

Lots of stuff that everybody in the United States took for granted could be considered a luxury item in Brazil, like phones, for example. Even people with good regular jobs who would naturally have a telephone in the United States might only be on a waiting list to get a phone here and that sometimes it cost over $500 to get a simple phone installed. That's because the phone company might have to put in a whole new line just to get you a phone because maybe nobody around you ever had one before. Still, it wasn't too bad for the unpoor people in Brazil who did not have a phone, because they still had empregadas and they could just send the empregada out to deliver messages instead of calling up. It was the same with other things lots of people have in the United States, like pocket calculators and air conditioners.

One thing I never found out was if the empregadas got bothered by the creepy guys when they went out to deliver messages or go to the store. I did find out, though, that lots of the empregadas never went to school and couldn't read or write at all. Most people didn't think it was very important for empregadas to read, but Mario's mother did. She gave the empregadas reading lessons every day. Mario's grandmother gave her empregada reading lessons, too, but it was not out of compassion. It was so the maid would not get cheated at the store.

On New Year's Eve Mario's mother gave both the empregadas the night off and the next day off. Mario's parents went to a fancy party with the other people from the Big

International Corporation. Mario's father wore a tuxedo, and his mother wore a long gown but she could not wear her fur stole because it was too hot.

Mario and his musician friends were invited to a very fancy party, too, given by some jet set people at a zillionaire's apartment at Copacobana. Even Eva Moreno was going to be there singing.

We decided not to get dressed up. I said that it wasn't very nice not to get dressed up if everyone else was, but the musicians said that no matter what we put on, if it was something we owned it wouldn't be good enough for them anyway, so don't even bother. So we all just went dressed as our normal selves.

I felt kind of weird walking into the jet set New Year's Eve party looking like my normal self; but the musicians were right, no matter what we would have worn, it wouldn't have been good enough anyway. All the jet set people looked just right. They were all wearing white clothing that showed off their suntans. I was the only person there who did not have a suntan at all, and that was because nobody would ever go to the beach with me because it was too hot, and because I spent the whole previous part of the winter in Boston and not on the Riviera or Copacobana.

The party was a terrible experience. Everyone was acting very snobby and speaking French. Eva Moreno asked Mario and his friends to play some music with her. It started out OK, but after Mario had been sitting at the piano playing for a few minutes, a creepy guy came up to him and tried to smash the piano cover down on Mario's fingers while he was playing.

About ten other guys joined in the fight, and finally somebody's body guard broke it up and we left. Mario was terribly mad, and then he got so drunk that we just had to come home. All he did then was walk around the apartment bumping into things from staggering around so much. He even broke a beautiful crystal decanter full of Grand Marnier that his mother had on a coffee table. It shattered into a million sticky, sharp pieces, and I had to clean them up all by myself.

Thank goodness Mario's mother wasn't around to see that. It would have upset her too much, but I was more used to it. It was sad to see that he was just the same, though, and that when anything bad happened, he'd just get drunk like always. It was a mess. Just like the old days of living with him. Just like always.

Nothing had changed.

After Mario passed out and I cleaned up all the glass and Grand Marnier, the phone rang. It was Mario's musician friends. They said was Mario feeling cheered up by now and did we want to go to the beach to the Macumba celebration. I said that Mario was passed out cold, but that I would like to go to the beach very much.

The musician friends thought it was kind of weird that I would go without Mario, but they came by and got me anyway, and then we went right back to the beach, the same beach that was right in front of the zillionaire's apartment building, the place where we'd just come from where there was still a party going on.

This time we did not go into the building, but we stayed outside at Copacobana, right out on the beach. What was starting to happen on the beach was very special. It was a Macumba New Year's Eve Celebration, a poor people's New Year's party.

Macumba is the pagan voodoo religion of Brazil, kind of. That's what you could think of it as. I don't know very much about it, but they know for sure that there are invisible spirits and vibrations that are real and alive and have invisible powers. Many other peoples of the world, mostly White peoples, do not know this. But the Macumba people have many gods and goddesses: of the ocean, and of different things in life and nature. They had pictures and statues and gourds and animal teeth, and brought many other things that they use in their religion.

The Macumba people at Copacobana beach had all their percussion instruments out on New Year's Eve, all their drums and gourds and things. They were making and dancing the real samba music, kind of like a voodoo samba, the real samba that people do for hours and hours until the rhythm of it puts them into the real power of the invisible vibrations surrounding them.

Dancing sambas with the Macumba people in Rio is one of the great experiences of life. It is fun and it is spiritually very intense, too, but not very many White peoples of the world know what this is like. It is like the whole world and all the people in it are throbbing together, in step together, combining their lives and their blood all together, and you can feel it throbbing, throbbing. And you can feel it in your body and you can feel it in your spirit. It is the spirit of all the peoples of the earth combining all of their energies into one dancing rhythm. It is all the energies of humanity uniting with God, the spirits, the invisible vibrations. It is everything together all at once, at one with each other.

But it is something that the White peoples of the world will not want to experience because they would find it frightening because it would not be compartmentalized or sanitary enough. But this spiritual, rhythmic dancing that the voodoo peoples of the world experience is a great and wonderful thing. And it is all I would ever want of life, all that I would ever ask of the world is that everyone, everywhere just stop what they were doing and dance the samba all together for fifteen minutes. It would change the course of history.

I guess the trouble for most people who aren't poor, who can read, who are educated, people who have washing machines or telephones or things like that, the trouble is that they wouldn't much be too welcome to the celebrations that the voodoo peoples of the world have, either, because those peoples are very poor and illiterate, and they know the harm that the wealthy classes of the world inflict on the poor peoples, and there is a lot of anger; and so the wealthy classes of the world would also have to let go of their money in order to come and join in with the voodoo peoples of the world so that everyone in every nation could dance together in the same samba rhythm.

Anyway, even though Mario and some of his friends had some bits of money, they could still be with the Macumba people and dance the samba because they had the real love of the rhythm and the spirit. The Macumba people let me dance with them, too, even though they stared at me because I was so pale. Most of them were very dark. The musicians told them I was a "Norte Americana." But even though lots of the Macumba people stared at me and wondered who I was, they did not act creepy to me.

I looked up behind me for a minute at the building where the jet set party was going on. It was full of rich people being snobby. They were not having too good of a time, but they preferred showing off their clothes and enjoying their expensive liqueurs.

I think that was the greatest moment of my life, the moment that I had been looking for, searching for, waiting for; and Mario was the one who got me there to this time and this place where I wanted to be, but now that I was there, just where I wanted to be, there with the voodoo samba music, where was Mario? Home at his Mom's passed out.

The next day, New Year's Day, Mario woke up with a terrible hangover. I had come in very late the night before, but he never even noticed that I was gone. I knew I might as well go back to Boston when I saw the weird look in Mario's eye. He just wasn't there any more. There was something weird in his eye, a weird look that I didn't know and didn't understand and didn't like, either. I can't describe it. It was just something. I figured that if I didn't go back to Boston soon, I'd be stuck there taking care of Mario for the rest of our lives while he got to be more and more of a real, true drunk.

I told Mario's father that I had to be getting back to Boston, with the help of a Portuguese-English dictionary. But Mario's father said, "What's the rush? Why don't you stay and go with us to the country house?" (well, something like that is what he said, with the dictionary.) I stayed a little while more.

The country house was a beautiful little stone cottage on the way to the Amazon Jungle in Rio Recife. Lots of rich people from Rio had little cottages at Rio Recife. There was even a sauna and a natural stone swimming pool where a natural little stream flowed in and out on its way somewhere else.

There was a family that lived in the caretaker's house on Mario's family's property. They had a daughter who was about thirteen years old. She was very cute and her name was Theresina. One day we decided to go into the little village and see a Walt Disney movie that was playing there, *1001 Dalmations*. Mario's mother asked the caretakers if they would like it if Theresina would come with us. Theresina's father said, no. He said she could not go because it was too sinful and she was not allowed to see things like that. Mario's Mom explained that it was just a Walt Disney children's movie and that it was not even serious or sinful in any way, but that it was just simple funny stuff for kids. Still, the man would not let Theresina go to the movie.

Mario's Mom told me that there were lots of people outside the cities in Brazil who thought that way, and that they could not read or write, and they would not let their children go to school, so that their children could not read or write either, just like the empregadas in the cities. We had to go to *1001 Dalmations* without the girl.

One day we took a drive in Mario's father's little car. We

went into the little village near the cottage. We looked all around, and the most interesting thing that I saw was a coffin shop. It seemed strange to me that there was a coffin maker who had an open air coffin-making shop right out on the sidewalk like any other open-air shop in the village. The coffin maker was just sitting there sanding his coffins. You could go right in and buy one and take it home if you needed to.

This is not something you would ever see in the United States. The United States is progressive in some ways, but not progressive about death. In the end there is not so much progress you can make about death. Everybody dies sooner or later and there's nothing you can do about it. Of course Walt Disney did have himself frozen when he died, in case they invented some way to cure the disease that he died of, or in case they figured out how to bring people back to life after they died when technology improved, some time off in the future. But he is one in a million. The rest just die.

I asked Mario if it were normal to have a coffin shop right out in the open and he said, yes, it was. He said that it was something everyone needed sooner or later and it was just a normal thing, and you could see coffin shops in Rio as well as in little villages like Rio Recife.

One night when Mario and I were sitting alone under a banana tree in back of the little cottage, I asked him if he didn't think that all that alcohol he was drinking would kill him if he didn't stop. He said, "Well, of course it's going to kill me. What do you think?" I said, "What are you talking about? Are you all ready to die or something already?" he said, "No, not at this precise moment," but that he would be ready to die in about five years because there wouldn't be anything left that he could do with his music then, by the time five more years went by.

I told him that he would change his mind in five years when the time for him to die came around, and he'd be all sick, and that he would not want to die at all when that time came around. I said, "It's not exactly as easy as you think, dying. You'll change your mind." But Mario said that *I* was the one who would change *my* mind when the time came around because I would understand then that there was nothing else that he could do with his music because technology was taking over the music business, too, and there would be nothing that he would have to offer. He said that even then hardly anyone wanted his music too much, and he could hardly afford to keep living as it was.

I hoped that he would get better and change his mind. One afternoon before I went home Mario and I stopped to have a coffee at a sidewalk cafe in Rio.

There at the cafe I finally saw these little children hanging around selling Chiclets, the orphan children that Mario had told me about before. They didn't have any shoes, and they were all dirty and ragged. Mario said that there were about a zillion more of these children, the ones that lived in rat holes with the creepy old guys. They'd walk around selling Chiclets, and then at the end of the day they'd give the creepy guys all their money.

Mario said why wouldn't any of these children want to be Communists when they grew up if they knew that they could get a good meal that way. That made me feel real weird, and I wondered why Mario wasn't a Communist, but he wasn't in a very good mood, and so I didn't want to ask him that question. It just would have made him madder.

Rio was a strange place. There was a lot more going on than naked belly-buttons and bikinis. A lot more. I didn't really like it much, though.

The next day Mario and his father drove me back to the airport. We drove past some beautiful beaches. We drove past the center of the city. In the center of the city, there were lots of soldiers, which you didn't see back around the beaches.

The soldiers were driving around in army trucks, wearing camouflage uniforms and carrying rifles or something. It was strange to see these soldiers in their uniforms, riding around in open trucks with weapons and everything. It was strange to see them in the middle of downtown on a nice, normal, hot day, when nothing special was going on.

Then we drove past the suburbs full of poor people, and then we were at the airport. That was the last time I ever saw Mario again.

About five years later, just as Mario had predicted, he died. He died of a mysterious tropical virus. I guess I might as well have stayed with him that whole five years because I kept thinking about him all the time and everything. I still think about Mario quite a lot now, even though he's dead.

But I guess one reason why I thought about Mario so much was that I admired how he could just sit there at the piano day after day, over and over, and never stop or give up. At least not till the end, I guess.

That's why I decided to write a book. I don't really know how to write a book, but I thought if I sat here long enough, like Mario, something would come out of me, out of my mind, out of my self, and into the air. I guess that in the end, everybody has to stop what they're doing and die; but before I die, I just want to see if I can make something out of thin air, like Mario did.

Epilogue

I guess this must seem like a pretty sad story. Sometimes I think, "Gee, if I had been smart and not left Brazil, I could be sitting under a banana tree with Mario right now." But even if I'd stayed there, it wouldn't have changed the fact that Mario was going to die.

It used to break me up something terrible, but now I understand why, why he died. He always used to say it was just because nobody appreciated his music, but that wasn't true. Lots of people appreciated his music. No, Mario died because he lived in between two worlds, and he couldn't stand the feeling of being split all the time.

And I don't just mean the two worlds of the United States and Brazil, either. Mario's two worlds were the rich world and the poor world. He didn't really belong in either one, but he suffered from the problems of both of them.

But the happy part of this story is when I went back to Phoebus to see Mom and Billy. I was at Billy's Bar-B-Que one day, just filling up the salt and peppers again, like always. And who do you think walked in? Big Mamma, the one who used to own the barber shop, the Black barber shop across the street. She looked just the same as ever.

It seemed very strange to me, how she just walked in so matter of factly and ordered a bar-b-que sandwich and a coke. Billy stopped and told her a stupid joke, just like he used to do with the old veterans in the old days. He never would have done that in the old days, though, because Black people never ever used to come into Billy's Bar-B-Que.

When she was ready to leave, she stopped and talked to me. She said, "Lands, child, aren't you the one who was always in here before, working away like there was no to-morrow? I used to see you through the window all the time."

I didn't know what to say, and so I just said, "Yes, ma'am," just like I used to say in the old days when I was there before. I didn't say anything else to Big Mamma, but in my heart, it was something special to me. I wasn't the only one who used to look across the street through the window. I just asked Billy, after Big Mamma was gone, why did Big Mamma come in now, when she never did before. Billy just said, "It's the new days now, honey. It's the new days."